Stories from Texas College Students

Charles Dickens, 1812-1870

Stories from Texas College Students

edited by

Gretchen Johnson

LITERARY PRESS
LAMAR UNIVERSITY

ISBN: 978-1-942956-23-5
Library of Congress Control Number: 2016936001

Portraits of famous fiction writers: each wrote
when about the age of the writers in this book.
  Charles Dickens, 1812-1870
  Jane Austin, 1775-1817
  Edgar Allen Poe, 1809-1849
  Lady Murasaki, c. 973 or 978 – c. 1014 or 1031

Lamar University Literary Press
Beaumont, Texas

For Story Tellers Everywhere

Fiction from Lamar University Literary Press

David Bowles, *Border Lore*
Kevin Casey, *Four Peace*
Terry Dalrymple, *Love Stories, Sort Of*
Gerald Duff, *Memphis Mojo*
Gretchen Johnson, *The Joy of Deception*
Christopher Linforth, *When You Find Us We Will Be Gone*
Tom Mack and Andrew Geyer, editors, *A Shared Voice*
Harold Raley, *Louisiana Rogue*
Jim Sanderson, *Trashy Behavior*
Jan Seale, *Appearances*
Melvin Sterne, *The Number You Have Reached*
John Wegner, *Love is not a Dirty Word and Other Stories*
Robert Wexelblatt, *The Artist Wears Rough Clothing*

For information about these and other LULP books, go to
www.lamar.edu/literarypress

Acknowledgments

I much appreciate the staff at Lamar University Literary Press for their ongoing hard work and support of the press and of this book.

Without the cooperation of the English professors across Texas, I would not have received the mass of submissions I was sent in order to see this project through. Thank you to each teacher who sent your students my way and helped them see their ambitions of publication realized.

And to all the students who submitted your work, thank you. This book is for you as well as for all readers who like a good story.

Jane Austin, 1775-1817

Foreword

The desire to tell a story, to put pen to paper in an attempt to encapsulate somehow the emotions surrounding a series of events, is no easy task. Many children hear stories even before they learn to speak, but it takes years to be able to create one's own stories and years beyond that to learn to create anything worth writing. For many writers, the college years are the period where talent, craft, and creation finally intersect. The stories chosen for this anthology have those three qualities.

When putting the anthology together, I was struck with the diversity of subject matter the college and graduate students across Texas are writing about. One story's narrator works as a professional snuggler. Another story sheds light on the realities faced by a child who is abused. In one story, the protagonist struggles with the emotional difficulty of saying goodbye to an old car, and in another story, poverty and the dangerous power of stereotypes serve as central themes. One of the greatest strengths of this anthology is its wide range of topics.

The desire to hear stories develops early, and it doesn't go away but usually changes form. Instead of furiously flipping through page after page of a night-time story we've read dozens of times, most of us transfer that love of fiction to the viewing of television sitcoms or blockbuster movies. But a few hold onto that need to sit down and read a story, to let the action play out in their own imaginations as words merge with their minds. And some even sit patiently and invent a plot and characters, figure out important things for those characters to say, and describe a reality that we all understand even if we've never stood there. The writers selected for this anthology are the ones who do just that.

Gretchen Johnson

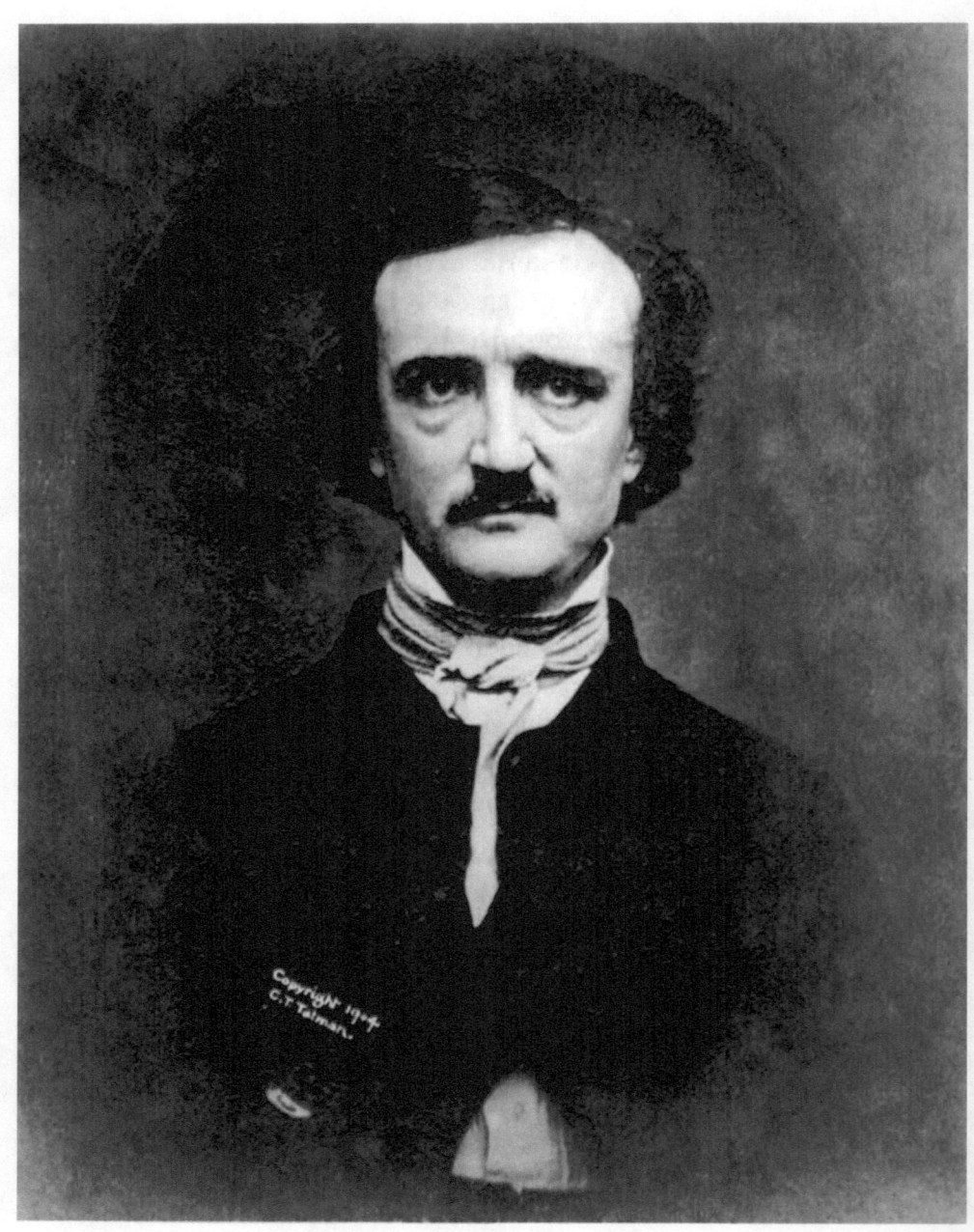

Edgar Allen Poe, 1809-1849

Contents

Lady Murasaki, c. 973 or 978 – c. 1014 or 1031

Looking Inside Tulips
Melissa Becker

I was supposed to save the world. That is, if you believed what mothers and psychics had to say—the only people guaranteed to tell a man exactly what he wants to hear. Although, I wasn't sure that really was what I wanted to hear; there are those who would have begged to differ. Callie, for instance.

The intermittent hum of the neon open sign in the window was enough to nauseate me those days. It wasn't that I had a sensitive stomach or anything annoying like that. I just really and truly loathed Green Street Motel. Then again, it wasn't really the motel itself; the work was easy, and the customers didn't hassle you too much. It was the lump of waste that ran it that made it arson worthy.

When I heard Chuck come in through the back, I hurried to finish putting out the "hospitality" breakfast. The idea of Chuck being hospitable made me laugh out loud. Pulling out the waffle mix, scoffing at the stupid, smiling sun cartooned on the front of the package, and checking that all the customers were gone, I added a little something from the small tube in my pocket before mixing and dumping the batter into the dispenser. A few months before, Chuck had made us start using this low fat, low carb mix because it was "healthier," and the irony was lost on everyone but me.

I made my way back behind the counter and waited. Looking around I wondered, not for the first time, how that place ever got any business. It was clear that the lobby used to be reasonably charming. From what I understood, Chuck's wife, Emily, had decorated it before he ran her off. I supposed she wasn't keen on sharing her husband with other women. That had been years ago, though. The paint had yellowed since then, and the wallpaper was peeling in places. What used to be cozy furniture had become scuffed and stained. The once decent floor-length curtains were drooping and pulling at the rods in what looked like an escape attempt.

Though we kept them clean enough, the rooms weren't much better.

I checked my watch three times and checked two customers out of their rooms while I sat waiting for Chuck, the only person who ate enough of my concoction for it to make a difference, to prance his sleazy ass in. He was probably busy Just-for-Men-ing his hair, or drowning in cologne, or doing bicep curls in the mirror. He liked to "keep his guns oiled and loaded," whatever that meant.

Soon the jingle of bells caught my attention as the entrance door swung open. Callie burst in waving something high above her head, careening toward the counter. She didn't usually come by this early, and I had no doubt that it had something to do with her current energy level. I checked my reflection in the window to my right. My almost-black hair was in a pseudo-pompadour because I knew she liked them, and I wondered if she'd say anything. I guess I liked it well enough. It kept my hair out of my "doe eyes," as Callie once called them, and I assumed it was a compliment.

When she reached the counter, she slammed the item she had been waving down in front of me so that I could see her name bold and wide across the top of a glossy oversized postcard. Callie Cunningham. "I got it! I got it, Tyler! McAllister is hosting my work. Finally!" Her chestnut brown cascade of curls had yet to stop bouncing from the trauma of her frenzied running. I studied her bright gray eyes, wild with fervor. I'm tall enough that Callie had to shift her gaze upward to look at me, and I liked it because her eyes caught more light that way.

"Awesome, Cal. I knew you'd wear him down," I told her through a sideways grin. I didn't add the part about it taking two years.

"The opening is next week, March fifteenth. Make sure you're available that night," she said through what could have been taken as a glare.

"Why the scowl? Of course I'll be there," I promised.

"Cross your heart and hope to die?"

"Step on a cat and spit in his eye," I finished our usual swear. Satisfied, she bounced back out of the lobby as quickly as she came, leaving the promotional postcard on the counter in front of me. I picked it up and studied the painting plastered across the front. It just looked like a bunch of flowers to me. What kind, I had no idea, but I've never been one inclined to the art of botany. They were quite pretty, though, I supposed. They were quite... perfect, actually. The colors were brilliant and seemed to speak. The petals seemed to glow, emerging from a bottomless darkness beneath them. Despite the darkness, however, I thought of sunshine, and I didn't know why. Suddenly, I couldn't remember if I was thinking about the painting or Callie and had to bring myself back to reality.

I pulled the schedule out of the top left-hand drawer and let out a breath that I didn't know I was holding. I was off on the fifteenth. After all, I didn't want to advocate animal abuse.

The chime of the telephone interrupted my thoughts. "Green Street Motel," I answered.

"And . . ." came my boss' voice on the other end. Every once in a while, Chuck would decide to give a shit. This time he had come up with this clever slogan that he wanted us to say when we answered the phone. I couldn't remember what it was, so—

"The cheapest hole around with a bad case of syphilis at no extra charge," I responded without thinking and immediately flinched. I asked myself, not for the first time, where the line was between pride and masochism. There was a click from the receiver and the squeaky groan of the office door's hinges.

"What the fuck, Tyler? You got your ass on backwards today?" Chuck began, before he was even fully out of his office. His puffy hands were held up, palms to the ceiling in exasperation. The spotty blemishing of them was both gross and satisfying. You see, one of the side effects of his sunshine waffles was swelling and discoloration of the skin. "It ain't that hard to find a monkey like you to run this desk," he continued. "So, please, keep on with your bullshit." Knowing that I needed the job, I didn't roll my eyes but settled instead for a raised eyebrow. After what he thought was sufficient time for an awkwardly soul-penetrating glare, his shoulders dropped, and his demeanor shifted.

"So, was that Callie I heard?" he asked in his slimiest voice, a grin spreading across his face. He walked toward me with his chest pushed out, like one of those birds that puffs up when it's trying to attract a mate, his yellowed eyes wide with bad intentions. Jaundice, I supposed, another fruit of my efforts. Though, if he had hepatitis, I would have been neither surprised nor upset.

"Yeah," I grumbled, "Too bad you missed her."

"Mmm. Yes, missed. That's the word," he said, and I waited for drool to spill over his bottom lip. It didn't. I chalked it up to the dehydration evident through his dry, cracking lips, and I kind of wanted to start a list of the things I'd taken away from him.

"Well, if she missed you, she would have stuck around. Take a hint," I mumbled. He seemed not to hear. Instead, he just made his way to the Texas-shaped waffle iron and filled it with batter. I noticed that his normally tight and showy button-up had started to slacken, and I smiled inwardly. Chuck used to be more fit than a pair of tailored pants. Temporarily satisfied, I made my way around my corner and toward the office Chuck had just left.

"Just a sec, Ponyboy. Gonna have to update the schedule. Until I can get another night-shifter, you're gonna have to pick 'em up."

"All of them?" I asked in a way that made it difficult not to drop my jaw.

"Yeah. I can't see shit anymore at night," he said, and I guess I really only had myself to blame for that. Nyctalopia is another side effect.

"And? Did you forget where the damn light switches are?" I asked. He ignored me.

"Darlene has kids; you don't. Michael has school; you don't. I'll get someone else, but it'll be a few weeks." He smothered his waffle with this liquid, fat-free butter stuff, and for some reason my mind was filled with the image of a crocodile's death roll when it drowns its prey before eating it. "See ya tonight," he said with complete indifference. As I turned to leave, one of Chuck's barely-legals sauntered in and sat down next to him. He muttered something about her needing a "fucking watch" and called her by a name that I was pretty sure no mother would give her child as I pushed open the door, and I was pleased that she got to watch him eat the sunshine waffles.

When I exited the motel, Callie was there waiting for me, nose deep in a tabloid she had picked up. Her face was hidden, but a light breeze rustled her chestnut curls so that they seemed to dance around the edges of the magazine, and I heard Tchaikovsky in my head. A stack of her fliers was sticking out of her purse. A pit rose in my stomach, and I was mad at Chuck all over again. Wordlessly and not looking up, she followed me down Green. After several minutes, she spoke, catching me off guard.

"Have you ever looked at the inside of a tulip?" she asked with a tone that one might use to ask if it were going to rain.

16

"Uh, no. I suppose I haven't," I replied.

"Isn't that always the way of it?" she said. Her nose scrunched a little, and her brow kind of furrowed. "Anyone can pick a tulip out of a line-up, but only if we see its profile. That's how we imagine them, isn't it? A little cup with a jagged top edge."

"Sure. I guess," I said and thought of her painting with no cups or jagged edges.

"I just think it's a shame," she continued. "There's so much more in there, and we don't even pay it any mind."

"Yeah. Hey. Don't take this—um— just don't come see me at work anymore, okay?" I had my gaze to the sidewalk with my hands shoved into my pockets. I turned to see her reaction. She looked at me like I'd sprouted a horn, then nodded.

"Chuck?"

"Chuck. I don't want to kill him any sooner than I have to," I said, wondering what she would think if she knew I wasn't joking.

"I think I can manage," she said through a giggle. "It's not that big of a deal. He'll give up eventually."

"And if he doesn't?" I asked.

"I'll just attribute it to his inability to know when to get lost. Really, it doesn't get to me. Ooh! In here!" she exclaimed as she tugged me into the shop to our left, and I wondered if it needed a new clerk.

The scents of incense and desperation assaulted me. Callie loved fortune tellers. She didn't believe them—she was too keen for that—but there was a novelty to them that amused her. While we were in there, she'd pretend to take everything to heart, giving her most sincere and sometimes grave reactions to the readings. I didn't have it in me to humor psychics, so I just didn't talk when she made them read me.

"This line here, how it crosses this one, this means you are destined for greatness," the medium's wrinkled and shriveled lips said as she studied my palm, though she didn't actually indicate which lines she was talking about. She babbled on about a destiny of ostensive heroism and morality. They always said something of that sort. Of all the psychic dealings, the palm readings were probably my favorite because they're the only ones really based on you. Not that this means they're any more accurate, but what the hell connection do some cards or a rounded piece of quartz really have to a person? Callie would probably say that palm readings were looking at the inside of the tulip instead of at the outside. She always said stuff like that. I just thought that the nature of them lent at least some sort of consistency.

When we left, Callie was abuzz with an ardent discussion of our "futures."

"So, what's your plan?" she asked me.

"Plan? For what?" I asked back.

"For saving the world," she said brazenly, as if it were obvious. Her silvery eyes stared at me with expectations of a genuine answer.

I truly started to think for a moment and then shook it off. "Cal, those people have no idea what they're talking about. They just say what you want to hear."

"Then what you're telling me is that you want to save the world. So what's your plan?" she repeated. This stunned me, and I paused. I guess that is what I said, though I'm not entirely sure it's what I meant. For whatever reason, I thought of Chuck.

"Well, I reckon I'll just eradicate one bad guy at a time," I replied with a grin. She answered it with a playful punch to my shoulder, and without realizing what I was doing, I answered that with a kiss on her cheek. She stared at me through slight confusion for a second, then giggled and told me she was going home.

Hoping to catch Michael and con him into working the fifteenth for me, I went back to the motel early. He had already left, though, so I sat in the office to brood. I didn't like that room much. It was cramped and smelled of stale coffee and menthol, and I couldn't decide if that was offensive or laughable. I scanned the room, and my eyes locked with a picture on the wall, as they always did, the one of Chuck and his wife that he never got around to taking down. Emily's image had an eerie presence, and, though we'd never met, she looked strangely familiar. My attempts to answer why were soon interrupted, however, when Chuck strutted in.

"Why're you here so early?" he asked as he made his way to the desk at the far end.

"Couldn't stay away," I said. He groaned as he plopped into the desk chair, clutching his forehead. It was the vertigo, and I reached into my pocket and gently tapped the vial as if rewarding a dog for good behavior. Pulling a metal flask out of a desk drawer, his trembling hands unscrewed the cap with difficulty, and he took a swig. The motor nerve damage was probably my favorite; it had to be the most debilitating.

"Well, since you're here, I think I'll go ahead and call it a day," he said. It figured. With a smug smile, he stacked his feet on the desk, trying to look invulnerable to whatever had a grip on him. I wanted him to leave so badly that I didn't even protest.

"Off you pop, then," I said and walked out of the office.

I walked into the lobby and saw a sloppy note taped to the front window. Through it I could read "Overnight Help Wanted" scribbled in shaky letters with a heavy black marker. Yep, the nerve damage was my favorite. With a sigh, I plugged in my headphones and leaned back in the chair behind the counter.

After about twenty minutes, I heard the telltale jingling of bells and raised my head to see a woman approaching the counter. Her olive eyes were deep, and her bleached hair could have used a brush. Her dress was too big, and her heels were too small. Her heavy earrings pulled at her ears like a desperate child tugging at its mother. If poignant had a look, she was it. As she traipsed up to the counter, I wondered what expression I was wearing.

"You Chuck?" she asked. You wish.

"Definitely not," I replied. "Back outside and to the left. Room 101." Why didn't he tell them this when he called? Was I supposed to be impressed? Jealous of the STDs he was soon to get? She left without another word, shuffling awkwardly in the too small heels.

After what was probably less than a minute, the bells rang again, and I figured Poignant was having trouble finding the place that no one should have trouble finding. When I looked up, however, Callie was standing in the door wearing a wide smile.

"Figured you could use some company. I know Tuesdays are your slowest nights," she said with her strongest puppy-dog eyes.

"I told you not to come up here anymore," I said, though I was happy to see her.

"Come on, what are the odds that Captain Ball-Buster is going to leave that room for the rest of the night? I saw his dinner order go in there," she said. "Ooh! Let's play 'The Creep and the Prostitute'!" She switched to a grumbly voice and slurred, "You're late, wench." She strutted over in a too-accurate-for-comfort manner, trying not to laugh as she did. "Now, take them panties off," she grunted and followed it with an awkward and creepy mm-hmm. Trying to contain the laughter myself, I readied myself to chime in for my part, when I was interrupted.

"The fuck are you two doing?" came a voice from behind us. We turned around to see Chuck standing in the office doorway. My stomach sank, and I wondered how much he had heard. A lump in my throat prevented any kind of immediate response to his question.

"Callie, so nice of you to visit me," he said as he slithered closer to her, his creepy grin revealing strikingly white teeth, and I wondered how he managed that between the cigarettes and coffee and arsenic. He put his arm around her shoulders, and my jaw clenched. "Congrats on the exhibit," he purred, and I'm pretty sure I tasted bile. "I wouldn't miss the opening for anything," he continued, ending it with a wink.

"Thanks," she said and smiled. She actually smiled. He turned and walked toward the counter. Grabbing his wallet out of a bottom drawer, he paused.

"Quit dicking around," he said to me with a short glare before he turned to leave. He pinched Callie playfully on the arm and gave her another wink as he walked out.

"Sorry," Callie said sheepishly after he was gone.

"Don't be," I told her. "I put your exhibition for the wrong date on the calendar," I said, hoping that it would make her laugh, and it did.

"I'll be working when you get off, so I'll see ya Thursday," she said as she bounced toward the door, her usual energy restored, not nearly as bothered as I was that I wouldn't get to see her tomorrow. It was then that it hit me. It was Emily. Emily, Chuck's wife, looked so familiar because she looked like Callie. It was subtle, and it was all in the eyes. Both had the gleam of polished gray river stones. Both were also soft, like a cloud that only threatens. Perhaps most strikingly, both possessed a quality that simply asked for *more*.

It wasn't long before the typical noises started from Chuck's room since it shared the wall with the front desk. As 6 a.m. rolled around, I started on the breakfast. I had been working up the courage all night. When I got to the stupid, smiling sun waffles, I dumped the entire vial into the mix. I stopped for a moment and wondered what Callie would say. Not that I thought she would miss him, but she had this thing about being "tolerant." Then I thought of Poignant, of Darlene, of Emily, and of anyone else that Chuck had breathed on and slammed the lid to the dispenser shut.

When he walked in, he didn't say anything, only made his predictable path to the breakfast bar and started filling up Texas. He was always more quiet after the evenings when he "ordered dinner," as Callie so quaintly coined it. I looked at him then, really looked at him. I thought of the picture on his office wall, and I wondered what Emily would think. I thought of the flask in his desk, and I wondered what Jack Daniels would think. In a way, he seemed to be begging me. His clumsy fumbling begged for pity. His ill-fitting clothes begged for understanding. His yellowed complexion begged for forgiveness. His ignorance begged for sympathy. Then again, I think it was just the tulip talking.

Once he sat down, I walked a straight path toward the front door. As discreetly as I could manage, I flipped the sign in the door so that passersby would read "closed," probably for the first time since Green Street Motel opened its doors. I clicked off the humming neon light, and it seemed to sigh at the relief. With one last glance at Chuck, I locked the doors behind me. "Death by Texas," was what I hoped the headlines would read.

The World Drops Beneath You
Sonny Bohanan

The red lights of the television tower pulsed on and off in the distance, a constellation of dying stars lined up single file, like good soldiers, to wink out in unison. James stared at the glowing embers and drifted along the edge of sleep as his father drove through the early-morning dark. Pop turned up the radio, as he always did for news of the war, and James' mind snapped to attention: Nixon had announced he would bring home 25,000 troops during the next year. A tingle of hope raised goose bumps on James' arms and the back of his neck. But it was gone in a moment as he understood that it would not erase the draft notice folded in his back pocket.

Riding to and from work in recent weeks, James had silently rehearsed how to tell Pop that his number had come up. When he tried to say the words, though, his throat closed up, choked with anger and the bitterness of having brought the war to his own door. Words were useless. They couldn't stop the chaos that seeped nightly from the television like poison gas—riots and political assassinations erupting across the nation, the latest wave of troop replacements disappearing into a jungle no one had heard of until it arrived in their living rooms.

As Pop drove, the darkness fled imperceptibly, leaving inky traces behind in the corners and shadows of things. He turned the pickup in at the job site, and the headlights picked out three men drinking from thermos cups at the concrete base of the tower. Pop and James usually arrived fifteen minutes early to drink coffee with them, but it was already five-thirty.

"Couldn't get Shorty out of bed, huh?" Stony said as they stepped out of the truck. His real name was Dwayne, but everybody called him Stony, or Stoner.

"You can see the boy needs his beauty rest," Pop said.

Wally, the boss, tapped his wristwatch once with his right index finger, which had been cut off at the middle knuckle twenty years earlier. "Let's get up there," he said, and the men put on their tool belts. When James was a kid, Wally would push the shortened finger into his nostril so it looked like he'd planted it three inches deep.

Pop said to James, "I want you to go up top this morning and attach these brackets for the co-ax cable." He opened a box to see that the brackets were the right size, then asked Wally, "Did you get the elevator working again?"

"Yeah, but we've got to run it from the ground," Wally said. "The wiring's crossed, and I couldn't get the damn thing straightened out. I'll have to get an electrician out here."

It was July 20th and already hot at sunrise. The men were working on Sunday because a series of spring tornadoes had knocked out power for more than a week, and they were behind schedule. They lost money when a job was late and had less than a month to finish the tower, which rose nearly 2,000 feet above the High Plains and would soon transmit the signal for the ABC affiliate in Amarillo.

James started to sweat—he had never been all the way to the top of the tower. The crew had installed the elevator only two days earlier. Until now, getting to the top had meant climbing the ladder hand over hand for 180 stories. Pop and Wally were the most experienced, and it took them thirty to forty minutes wearing their tools. The elevator's steel mesh cage could do it in four minutes, but only two men could fit inside it.

"You want to ride on top?" Pop asked his son.

"I don't think so." James had seen Stony and Gilvin ride on the roof of the elevator several times. Except for James they were the youngest and were relegated to the shit jobs. Every newbie started at the bottom and stayed there until he could challenge the man above him, and win. Some never could.

"It's safe," Pop said.

James glanced inside the elevator at the loose wires sticking out of the control box but said nothing.

"Hell, he's scared," Stony said. "Me and Gilvin will do it." They climbed onto the roof, and James carried the box into the cage underneath them. Wally stepped in beside him.

Pop stayed on the ground to run the elevator. He lifted a walkie-talkie to his mouth, and the one on Wally's belt squawked.

"Let's go up." Pop punched a button, and the elevator lurched, rising slowly at first, then faster through the alternating red and white sections. James' stomach tightened as the world dropped beneath him. From below, the guy-wires that tethered the tower to massive concrete footings were taut, inch-thick cables that cut a straight line from ground to tower. But from above, James saw that the cables in fact drooped in tremendous arcs, all the tension the crane could muster unequal to gravity's ghastly force. The sight gave him a sick feeling. The laws of physics, so straightforward on the ground, were warped and unreliable at this height. He reached behind him and secretly laced his fingertips through the steel mesh.

The rush of the elevator cooled the sweat on his forehead. A haze of clouds permitted him to look directly at the sun, deliciously pink like a scoop of neon ice cream sizzling and melting along the bottom where it sat on the horizon. Wally spoke into the walkie-talkie, and the elevator stopped. He stepped out of the cage, and James' stomach swam as he followed. James held tightly to the steel beside him and stepped cautiously off the small elevator platform onto an 18-inch I beam.

Wally lowered himself into a sitting position and straddled the beam, his legs dangling on either side. Showing James what to do, he marked the steel with chalk, drilled four holes, and quickly attached one of the brackets with metal screws. He finished in a couple of minutes and handed the drill to James.

"We need one every ten feet," he said. "Just work your way down. Go ahead and do one, and I'll watch."

James attached the drill to his belt and stepped down the ladder. He was sweating profusely, soaking his T-shirt as he awkwardly worked the tape measure.

"Take you all day to do one," Stony said, amused, watching from atop the elevator.

James avoided looking at the ground while he measured ten feet and marked the holes. He barely got the leverage he needed to drill through the steel by clamping his legs to the beam, holding on with his left hand and drilling with his right. He took a socket wrench from his tool belt but fumbled it, made a swipe for it and missed, nearly losing his balance. Wally cupped his hands to his mouth and shouted, "Headache!" The wrench clanged twice against the steel as it fell, then, seconds later, a third time. The tiny dot on the ground that was Pop dove for cover under his pickup truck.

James looked up quickly to see if Wally would berate him.

"Here, you can use mine," Wally said, handing his wrench down to James. "Looks like you got the hang of this. We're going down to 1,500—we'll come get you at lunch."

James felt better with no one watching, but he was deadly slow. When he looked at his watch, an hour had passed, he had attached five more brackets, and his clothes were soaked. Until this moment, he'd never sweated through his jeans. He rolled his neck and shoulders to unkink the muscles and wondered how he would be able to keep at this for eight hours.

He had carried the draft notice for weeks because he didn't want Pop or anyone else finding it at home. Mom already knew. She had studied the envelope the day it arrived in the mailbox, and she handed it to James, unopened, while Pop was getting cleaned up after work. James asked her not to tell Pop.

"I want to be the one to do it," he said.

He had rarely seen Mom lose her composure, but she did then, after worrying about the letter all day.

"I told you not to quit school," she cried in a small voice that cut him to the bone.

"I told you, I told you, I told you," she sobbed through clenched teeth, hitting him in the chest with the edges of her fists each time she repeated the words.

As he worked his way down the tower, James decided that the worst had already happened—he would be in Vietnam by the end of the year—and the thought made him reckless. He imagined simply leaning forward and allowing himself to tip over the edge of the tower, spinning downward and being battered against the steel like his socket wrench.

How would he react in the face of death? He had avoided thinking about it, but at this moment, a week before he was due for his physical in Oklahoma City, he couldn't stop thinking about it. When Mom had handed him the letter, his first thought was to run, or simply to refuse. Either one would land him in jail. James decided he wouldn't tell Pop anything about the letter. Doing so would have forced Pop to confront the depth of his son's fear, and his weakness.

About eleven o'clock, the elevator climbed to the spot where James was working. He took perverse pleasure in walking to the cage without holding on.

"Damn, boy," Stony said. "Looks like you been swimming in them clothes."

Wally said, "You want to ride down with me?" He was standing on top of the elevator, and Stony and Gilvin were inside it.

"Sure." James got on top of the cage. He held onto the cable that lifted and lowered the elevator as Wally spoke into the walkie-talkie, and they started down.

James relaxed while the elevator gained speed. To the north he could see the Canadian River breaks, canyons of dark red and brown cut into the vast mesaland of the Llano Estacado. At that moment, the elevator jolted to a hard stop, and James grabbed desperately onto the cable with both hands, and his knees buckled. In the stunned silence, the only sound was the wind singing through steelwork.

After a couple of seconds, Wally lifted the radio to his mouth. "Pop, what the h—"

He didn't have time to finish. The world blurred as the elevator cage dropped again, free falling. It stopped abruptly, and James and Wally crumpled to their knees, clinging to the cable.

"You OK?" Wally asked.

It took James a moment to understand they were still hundreds of feet above the ground, unharmed. Wally stood up just as the elevator started down again, and James cringed, fearing another free-fall. He tried to stand as the elevator picked up speed, but his legs were shaking too badly. When they reached the bottom, Pop watched him get unsteadily to his feet. Stony and Gilvin stepped out of the elevator and followed Pop's gaze as James lowered himself, trembling, down the ladder.

"You all right, son?" Pop asked. James thought he saw Pop stifle a smile. When the other men laughed, James became furious and suspected that they'd planned to scare him. He walked to the truck, grabbed his lunch sack, and tried to ignore their chuckles as he sat by himself under a tree and ate.

* * *

James had refused to go to school when they moved to Texas after Christmas. He had worked the previous four summers and most of the school year, too, in each place they'd lived. But he was unable to find a job in Amarillo, and Pop suggested he help out on the tower crew. It was familiar work. When he was too young to get a paying job and his sisters were still very young, James went to work with his dad several times each summer, probably at times when he proved too much of a handful for his mother.

They'd lived so many places James couldn't remember all of them, and he was two years behind in school—eighteen years old and yet to start his junior year of high school. He didn't reveal his age to classmates. When they moved to Amarillo, he had wanted nothing more than to get a job and get the hell away from Mom and Pop, away from the travel trailer they'd hauled behind the pickup and on to the next job every six months for a decade. He was sick of being the new kid at school, of sleeping on the living room floor with his sisters, and of the shame of waking to find his underwear encrusted with the sex he knew only in his dreams. He considered morosely that he'd gotten his wish and would soon be gone.

The previous Sunday, Pop had let James take the pickup for the day. James drove it north of the river into the vast nothingness of the plains. During the spring, he had been mesmerized by the thunderheads that approached from the west and slid down the front slope of the Rocky Mountains, anvils on the horizon that built to mushroom cloud explosions he could see from 200 miles away. The storms arrived hours later, fast and violent, tearing off roofs and driving cattle into the pasture corners, crushed against barbed wire. His trip north of the Canadian was the farthest James had ventured since arriving in Texas, and he drove the back roads until he lost his way. Ahead he saw a windmill by the side of the road; it had been erected on top of a dirt mound about eight feet tall. He stopped the truck and climbed the little hill to read the historical marker. It explained that the area had been called no-man's land until the 1870s because the first white explorers had been routinely wiped out by thirst, Comanches, blizzards, and their own panic at becoming lost in a featureless moonscape untouched by human reckoning. James stood on the man-made hill and turned in a slow circle, scanning the horizon for 360 degrees.

Not a single tree or landmark. Not a building. The creases in the land, the canyons and river breaks that cut through the caprock, were hidden until you stumbled upon them. A sea of dry grass flowed wave after wave in the wind, speaking in a ceaseless dry whisper that spooked him, telling him he was alone in a world that had always been here and always would be, long after he was gone.

* * *

When the sun went down that Sunday evening after work, the men and their wives sat in lawn chairs on the little square of concrete outside Mom and Pop's trailer. Several pickup trucks were squeezed into the tight space between the patio and road. After everyone had eaten hamburgers, Pop carried the television outside and tuned it so they could watch the moonwalk. The little kids were nearby, the boys driving toy cars and trucks through the dirt, and the girls playing inside. James sat with the adults, drinking beer and ignoring their conversation so he wouldn't miss Neil Armstrong's first steps on the moon. He glanced from the television to the crescent moon suspended in the night sky and squinted, focusing intensely and hoping to see a tiny dot where the moon lander was. On the TV, Armstrong was waiting for the cabin pressure to stabilize so he could open the hatch of the module. He talked to the controllers in Houston, and they hurried him, urging him on. Static roared through the audio, punctuated by electronic beeps. At last the module opened, and Armstrong began his descent, stepping backward down the ladder, observing aloud on the fineness of the moon dust and comparing it to talcum powder. A wrinkle in the wavelength sent a ghostly moan across the universe, causing the hairs on James' body to stand on end as a chill ran through him, until finally, in an instant of faith, Armstrong stepped off the bottom rung, and his left foot touched the moon.

He must have planned ahead what he would say, James thought, as Armstrong said, "That's one small step for man, one giant leap for mankind." Moments later he left the first footprints in this new world, unchanged for millions of years and now colonized by America. James felt an emptiness when Armstrong planted a flag on the moon's surface. There was nobody to take the moon away from, no race of aliens or moon men to eradicate, so the flag would remind latecomers that we arrived first and came in peace, unless they try to take the moon away.

Armstrong bounced in the lesser gravity and stumbled once but didn't fall. James was surprised at the utter blackness of the sky behind him, stark against the daytime side of the moon. Later, Armstrong pointed the camera toward Earth, and James saw it from the astronauts' vantage, large and brightly colored with blue, green, white, and brown swirls, suspended in infinite night. James understood for the first time the darkness that shrouded everything, and he wondered how the astronauts didn't crack up. That was the fascination, to see whether they could find their way back home, and if they did, whether they retained a shred of sanity. And if they didn't . . . .

He imagined standing where Armstrong stood on the dead satellite, gazing homeward through the void as his air expired, or being driven mad when a jammed thruster set him spinning, weightless, forever. The futility struck James—it's lonely whether you go to the moon or don't go to the moon, so why bother?

He looked away from the TV as Stony's wife, Winette, explained drunkenly that the landing and the moonwalk were a hoax.

"I heard they're doing it in a movie studio. See, you can tell from the shadows. Look how fake they are." She pointed to the television, where Armstrong was in fact making long shadows, doing bunny hops in the slow-mo of one-sixth gravity.

"It's not fake," James said. "Why would they go to the trouble to fake a moon landing?"

"To stick our thumb in Russia's eye, why do you think, dummy?" Winette said. Stony became interested when James piped up.

"What's the matter, PeeWee? You have a rough day?" Stony said in a baby voice.

"He nearly died, you know," Stony continued to the others on the patio. That got Mom's attention.

"What?"

"He didn't nearly die," Pop said, his voice filled with weariness at the insinuation. "There was a short in the elevator, and it dropped a couple of inches, that's all. The brake kicked in, just like it's supposed to."

Anger brought James out of his shell. "It wasn't two inches that it fell." His voice was shaking. "And it wasn't a fucking short. You did that on purpose." He'd never cussed Pop before.

"The hell I did," Pop said.

"You made the elevator drop while James was in it?" Mom said, frowning at her husband. "I can't believe you."

"I just told you I didn't." His menacing tone was meant to end the discussion.

"He wasn't *in* the elevator; he was on top of it," Stony said, tipsy and oblivious to the effect of his words. "You should have seen him shaking when we got off the elevator."

Stony stood up as he warmed to his story, made his legs quiver and strutted like a chicken, eliciting giggles and a quiet ripple of laughter from the others. "Couldn't hardly even walk! I don't think you're going to make no ironworker, boy."

"Like I want to be a fucking ironworker," James shouted.

"That's good, 'cause we don't take pussies like you," Stony said. He laughed and made his legs shake again.

James stood and crossed the patio. Without thinking, he lowered his right shoulder and drove it into the older man's gut and wrapped his arms behind Stony's legs, driving him to the ground. Stony landed flat on his back, forcing the air out of his lungs, and James was on top of him. He grabbed James' face and gouged it, trying to get his eyes. They rolled in the dirt and underneath Pop's pickup truck. James wound up on top and grabbed the older man by the throat, bouncing his head between the ground and the transmission case. James felt the fight go out of Stony, so he scrambled from beneath the truck and stood next to it, ready to go again. When Stony crawled out his nose was pouring blood, and he put his hand up to ward off James.

"Hey, we're cool, we're cool." The men laughed unmercifully when they noticed his nose was broken.

James walked away quickly. He turned toward the trailer park exit and walked until he'd stopped sweating and his breathing had returned to normal. His shirt was ripped, and his face and elbow were bleeding. The knee was torn out of his jeans, which were stained with dirt and blood. He brushed off his clothes and looked up to find the moon, but it was hidden now, swallowed by a thick stand of oak trees that surrounded the trailer park. The sky was empty, black. He started walking again. He had no idea where he was going. Outside the park gate he left the road and walked into the trees.

Dust

Alaina Bray

Lilith froze. She turned back to consider the town for a moment.

She stood on a hill just within its borders, the only break in the flattened landscape. Elevated, she saw the lamps and lanterns of Charming flicker out as it put itself to sleep—electricity a fad that had not yet reached the town. Only a few windows still glowed; most of Charming's residents were long asleep, preparing for another day of farming the cotton that would not grow except in small, bedraggled patches like the spots of fur left on a dog with mange.

She turned her back to the city once again and lifted her foot to take her next step. She stopped, left the foot poised in the air, feeling as though there was something sacred and forbidden in the step—that this dirt, though only a single step farther than the dirt she had trod before, was what her father had always warned her about. This was dirt walked upon by immoral reprobate whom her father said awaited her outside of Charming. Charming abided no such wickedness. The outsiders, the ones not to be trusted who robbed banks with tommy guns and refused to remove their hats when meeting a lady, behaved this way.

Lilith brought her foot down to rest next to the other—in Charming. She sighed. Her father would smirk if he had been watching her, proud to know his warnings had chipped their way into her skull and burrowed through to the center of her brain, where like ear-wigs they snuggled quite contently in her mind, laying eggs and occasionally out of sheer boredom raising their pincers to sting pieces of the soft, pink mass.

But her father, of course, did not know she was here, so he could not share his satisfied smirk. He was resting within the wooden walls of their home, a home that stood alone among acres of empty cotton fields. He lay peacefully underneath the tin roof and faded quilt in a bed next to Lilith's faded mother.

His teeth were like millstones in Lilith's presence, grinding to-gether and eroding like the Oklahoma topsoil he could not keep from blowing away. Lilith's mother could sometimes hear the scraping as they sat in church where Lilith, lacking the proper air of seriousness, smiled in such a way that her nose crinkled while she sang along with the congre-gation to the slow cadence of the hymns.

Once, with the last chords of "I'll Fly Away" still resting in the air, Lilith had sung on, unnoticed at first—by all except her father, whose teeth had been grinding furiously between stanzas of his own singing. It took several moments for the echoes to fade from the whitewashed walls and for the rest of the congregation to realize not everyone had stopped singing. It was a realization that came slowly, people turning their heads to see what their neighbors were looking at, starting with the families sitting around Lilith and rippling from this center to the edges of the church until each dusty face was turned towards the girl who had not gone silent with the music.

Lilith stood with her eyes closed and her palms upturned, swaying peacefully to the sound of her own humming. The corners of her lips turned up into a brief smile as the words "Fly Away" came out in a half-breathed whisper and rounded with the murmur of "O Glory...I'll fly away." The other words were swallowed by a hum that emanated from her throat like the sound of distant train horns at night.

Those sitting closest could make out the words. Others felt only the hum and its weight, but they were enough to keep them enraptured in the thin, blonde spectacle. Men stood stony faced, some clenching straw hats in the leather of their hands. Women fidgeted next to their husbands, looking at the wood floors when the men glanced toward them and then, with a swallow, quickly back to Lilith. Those Lilith's age appraised her, running their eyes from the curls tied back messily with a ribbon to the bare feet that poked out beneath her faded floral print dress and the cracked leather shoes lying next to them. Many mimicked the expressions of their fathers, and the rest found themselves humming secretly, inaudibly along with her. The children, amused, watched with the same attention and affection they'd have given a stray dog doing tricks in the street.

Lilith's eyes squeezed tighter, as if in pain, as she half-hummed, half-sang the last words, "Hallelujah by and by. I'll fly away." Then she opened her eyes and lowered her palms back to her sides. Blood pooled pink in her cheeks, but she made no other acknowledgment of her audience other than a raise of her chin and a slow sweep of eyes across those who stared. Folding her body into the wooden pew, she started a ripple much like the last one, and those nearest to her sat down first with the rest following, sitting uneasily in the hard seats and hard silence.

It was then that Lilith's father chipped his tooth: the bottom left molar, second farthest from the back. His wife heard the crack and turned. Lilith looked resolutely forward as the preacher shuffled to the pulpit in his wilted suit and cleared his throat, unsure whether to begin. Drops of sweat were already beading on his pink, spotted forehead. Lilith's father spat out the fragment as he would a sip of sour milk and caught it in his hand. He looked at it, at Lilith, and back again and curled his lips in disgust at one of the two.

When the preacher had decided to speak, he began uneasily, quite aware that the congregation was still occupied with the sway and the hum of a farmer's daughter. But the farmer himself looked not at Lilith nor the preacher but at the fragment of tooth in his hand and rolled it steadily between the calluses of his thumb and forefinger until the service ended and the people filed, heads down in eager whispers.

The tooth's ivory interior contrasted with its surface, yellowed with the well water and the food the man had been too tired to brush away after nights of plowing, sowing, reaping under the Oklahoma sky. He came in only when dusk had begun to claim the plains and the Mexican free-tails joined him on the fields, gliding by his head and through the rows of cotton like dancers. He was fond of the bats many years ago, knowing they hunted the flies and mosquitoes that plagued him as he worked. He called them "My own personal farm hands," and when Lilith was a toddler, he would carry her outside, just after her mother had bathed her and dressed her for bed, pulling his reluctant wife too along by the hand.

"Jasper, you're going to get her dirty."

He would smile—his teeth so white, so charming then. "We have to see the bats, Lila Beth. The girl wants to play." He waited for the toddler's affirmation—a giggle or an eager tug on the straps of his overalls—and turned back to his wife. "Have a heart."

"Your food will get cold."

He would sit at their table and place Lilith on his lap. He made a game of seeing how fast he could eat the food, much to his daughter's delight. He grabbed handfuls of whatever Lila Beth had made him that night—chicken, beans, even steak on the best of nights—and shoved them into his mouth.

Lila Beth turned away so he wouldn't see her lips turning up at the corners. "Jasper, look at yourself! She is never going to have manners if you behave like that."

He looked to Lilith and pretended to snarl with his mouth full. She shrieked with laughter at his growls.

"Pa is a bear!" she would announce to her mother who was still turned away, the edges of her frown twitching and threatening to lift.

"Hear that, Jasper? You're a bear."

He chewed and swallowed as quickly as he could manage and rose, setting Lilith on the floor to go wipe his hands if the dinner had been messy that night. "Makes her laugh, though. Doesn't it, Lila?"

"Suppose it does."

He scooped up his daughter again and wrapped a hand around Lila Beth's slender wrist to lead the pair outside.

There in the fields, Lila Beth already abandoning her pretense of crossness, they would wait for the bats to dance by their heads. "Shhh," the father prompted, his daughter trying to stifle her giggles. Then, after moments of smiling anticipation, one of the creatures would pirouette by. Lilith would answer with a shriek of laughter, and her father would fake shock each time.

"You sound like a bat! Are you a bat?"

"Yes!"

"You're a bat? You're a bat!" He would lift her above his head, ignoring the soreness in his arms, and run with her through the rows of the then thriving cotton. She spread out her arms, flapped, and shrieked. Lila Beth chased them, but never quite fast enough. She caught her breath between strides and laughs.

"Jasper! Jasper, slow down! I'm not wearing shoes."

Jasper's soreness was less easily ignored later when the cotton came less easily and the top soil and the wind began to run away together like forbidden lovers—and when they found Lila Beth would have no more children. He grew too tired to do anything after his day in the sun and wind except come in and kiss the heads of his wife and daughter. And later, he grew too tired even for this. Their twilight dances with the bats became a memory for the father and a ghost of a memory for his daughter.

Lilith barely remembered the origin of her unusual habit years later when she continued with it and her father had long abandoned it. At twelve, she no longer shrieked and ran with the bats but waited with her arms out until they twirled around her as casually as if she were a tree. She watched them spin and open their mouths to emit the sounds that gave them sight. She liked to think they were singing.

Sometimes, her father would stare from where he worked in the field, but she learned to ignore him as he had done to her. He had once looked like his daughter, both of them fair-skinned and light-haired. But his pale skin had been tanned and leathered with the sun and wind, and his head of thick, yellow hair had thinned like the crops, a little more each season.

Then the storms began to carry away the soil like charmers carry away young daughters. The farmers began to wear Charming's dust in their hair and on their shoulders. Later still, in their eyes and in the hollow echoes of their laughs.

During one of the first storms, Lilith was sitting at the small wooden table in their kitchen, absorbed in sixth grade arithmetic home-work. Her mother sat next to her, peeling potatoes and occasionally looking at the school work she could not understand.

"You understand that, Lilith?"

"Yes ma'am, Mamma." Her mother nodded and smiled slightly as she looked back to her potatoes. Lilith's father, driven in early by the wind and dust, opened the front door and walked without a word towards the biscuits and beans waiting for him at the opposite end of the table.

Then he noticed the Mexican free-tail that had flown in behind him, it too seeking shelter from the storm. The three of them stared at the bat while it flew in panicked circles, realizing it preferred the storm to being trapped within the house. It shrieked and flapped its wings near the wall, hoping the sound would show it an escape. Slowly, Jasper turned away from the plate and followed the bat with his eyes. He walked with heavy steps toward the wall and extended his arm, waiting for the bat to come near. He swatted for it with an open hand when it flew within his reach.

"Jasper?" his wife whispered. She swallowed as he followed the bat into the middle of the room when it flew away from the wall. "Jasper, what are you doing?"

Lilith, misunderstanding, pushed back from the table and left her seat to join him, believing they were dancing like they had in her memory-ghosts. She stood by his side and held her arms out as he did, waiting for the bat to come near. She answered the bat's shrieks with laughter and began to twirl around Jasper, mimicking the circles the bat flew around his head, and, for a moment, she almost remembered how she and her father had once looked alike.

When the bat came near his face, he grabbed it by the corner of its wing and spun to the floor. Before it could rise, he stomped it twice with the hard bottom of his boot.

"No!" Lilith dived towards him. He stopped her, his large hand catching her at the chest, and turned to face her. His lips curled, and she was silent. The dust settled in the creases of his face made him look so much older. Dust from his boots powdered the bat's fur. Its ribcage was crushed. Its bottom jaw hung limp and sideways, and its small tongue poked out from the side. The membrane of its left wing had been torn as it was hurled to the ground.

Jasper took a deep breath through his nose. Then he kicked the kitchen wall and made his way back to his bedroom and slammed the door. Lilith knelt in silence over the small, broken form, and her mother, after a swallow and a sniffle, turned back to her potatoes.

The storms in those days were smaller and did not last as long. And when the wind and dirt had stopped swirling outside, Lilith's father emerged from his room. Wordlessly he scooped up the crumpled body that lay next to his daughter and carried it outside.

She remained on her knees for a moment, fingering the spot of blood where the bat had been, then rose to follow him outside.

"Lilith, maybe you shouldn't—" her mother started softly. Her words were lost as the screen door slapped shut.

It took her several moments to find him in the dying light. She spotted his hunched over form in one of the clusters of cotton that remained in the field, shaking in sobs. He held the body of the bat, running his thumbs over its chest that was matted with dust and blood.

"Pa . . ."

Jasper gasped and rose quickly. He wiped his face, smearing it with dirt and traces of blood. He lifted his arm above his head and cast the bat's

36

crumpled form into the shadows. Lilith followed its arc and watched it land, more crumpled now, in a small cloud of dust.

Jasper turned to face his daughter with a steel in his eyes.

"Lilith, you won't be going back to school tomorrow. You're going to start helping me in the fields."

"Pa . . ."

"Don't talk back, Lilith."

"Pa, please no." Her voice fell to a whisper. "I can't do that. I can't do that, Pa."

He stared at her for a moment and then turned for the house.

"Pa!" She followed after him, his steps quickening. "Pa!" He was already locked in his bedroom when she entered the house. She kicked the same spot on the wall he had, three times, bruising the tips of her bare toes. "Pa! Pa! Pa!" The word emphasized each kick. A sob swelled in Lilith's throat. She dug her fingernails into her palms and swung once at the air.

"Lilith? Lilith, what's happened?" Her mother's voice startled her. She had forgotten she was still in the kitchen.

"I'm not going back to school." She hated the sound of the words. "I'll be working in the fields."

Lila Beth looked down at the open arithmetic book and ran her hand over it, and a tear glistened at the corner of her eye as she closed it. She rose and put away the potatoes before walking to Lilith. Cupping her daughter's chin in her hand, she ran her thumb over her cheekbone with a sigh. "I'm sorry, Lilith." She kissed her on the forehead and turned for her bedroom.

Lilith paced the floors and dug her fingernails deeper into her hands. Bile rose in her throat when she glanced at the closed book. Her tooth dug into her lip until it tore the soft tissue and she detected the metallic taste of blood. She spit on the floor and hoped her father would step in it in the morning. Then she thought of her mother cleaning it up and turned to get a towel. Leaning down to wipe the blood-speckled froth, she noticed the drops of the bat's blood sprinkled on the floor next to her own. Before she could think about it, she ran her finger over the drops, smearing them into her saliva and blood. She paused and looked at the crimson on her finger and on the floor, and a tear dripped off her nose into the mixture. She stared at it for a moment before wiping it up, then rose.

Her feet carried her towards the door, into the dark. They brought her to the bat. One wing was completely broken now, twisted behind its head. She dug a shallow grave with her hands, dirt caking under her fingernails, and twisted a small cross out of twigs. Gently lifting the bat off the ground, she set to work picking mats of blood out of its fur and spat in her hand to clean off the powder of dust. She folded the creature's wings until they looked right again, careful not to tear them further. The bat stared back at her with glassy eyes and mouth hanging open, as if she were mesmerizing it. Lilith shuddered at the sight, closed its eyes and straightened its jaw, carefully putting the small tongue back in place. Then she gently kissed its head, placed it in the grave, and covered it with dust.

It felt wrong to leave, but she could think of no words, no eulogy to utter over it. She sat for a few minutes, then began to sing the only song that seemed to fit. Her voice was unlike a child's in the night's warm air, as if her twelve-year-old body housed the voice of a woman.

"I'll fly away, O Glory...I'll fly away. When I die—Hallelujah by and by. I'll fly away."

The Mexican free-tails accompanied her song, dancing near her and shrieking to the background melody of the cricket chirps. Lilith did not want to go back into the house, but tomorrow she would rise early to be with her father.

Each day for six years—except for the days of the storms that had begun to grow larger, blacker, carrying more and more of Charming's soil away—she rose and worked in the fields that grew more bare each season. The steel she saw in her father's eyes and the dust in the creases of his face never went away after that night. And though her skin never leathered the way his had, she grew leaner, thinner from the work and the meals that were also growing smaller.

On Lilith's eighteenth birthday, a week after her father had chipped his tooth, the family sat at the wooden table, eating dinner together. A storm had driven Lilith and Jasper in early. Lila Beth had given her own portion of rice and beans to Lilith as a birthday present. Her mother said little, as had become her habit.

Lilith looked at the empty plate in front of her mother.

"Pa." He looked up from his plate. "We can go to California. Like the others are doing."

He sighed and looked again to his food.

"Pa."

"We are not talking about this, Lilith."

She shook her head, pleading. "No!"

Jasper's worn hands dropped the fork, and it clinked as it bounced against the plate. "Lilith, do you know what kind of people are in California?"

She met his gaze, and her eyes narrowed. "Do you?"

"No!" His voice cracked as he pushed himself back from the table and stood. "I don't. This," he motioned with his left arm. "This," he stomped the floor, "is what I know."

Lilith too rose, picked up her mother's empty plate, and threw it before his feet. "It is killing us."

He stared at the broken pieces, and, for a moment, his body almost shook the way it had that night with the bat. He blinked slowly. Then, kicking the wall on his way out, he stepped out of the kitchen and away from his daughter.

A daughter who now stood, filled with resolve after the fight, both feet together on the border of Charming, considering the difference between its dust and the dust she was too afraid to place her feet upon.

She squatted to better see it, letting the hems of her cream-colored cotton dress touch the ground, kiss it. She sniffed the night air and then extended her neck, which seemed to glow in the fullness of the moon, over the forbidden dirt and drew another cold breath through her nose, hoping to discover a difference between the air of Charming and not-Charming. She liked to think she had detected one—that the air hovering over the forbidden dust hinted faintly at the smell of fruit that had just begun to overripe.

Then, her neck still extended over not-Charming, she lowered her back and brought her head closer to the ground. The tips of her blond curls touched its dust. Lilith swallowed. She lifted her left hand and let it hover in the air of not-Charming, paused, and felt for a difference. This air was perhaps thicker, filled with the pollen of the forest she faced and with a hint of the smoke of the city beyond it. Her hand drifted down gently and touched the dust with the tip of its middle finger. It felt different. She brought the other four fingers down, each landing softly on the dust like the lips of a mother on a newborn child. She drew the fingers slowly back toward her body and Charming, letting them trace patterns in the wonderful new dust, and then forward again. The new dust stuck to the tips of her fingers, coloring them with its lovely red-brown.

Then she fell to her knees, unconcerned about staining the cotton of her dress. The dirt made it seem even lovelier. She brought her other hand, without hesitation this time, to meet the dust and pushed it down with the full force of her palm. She curled her fingers and scraped the ground of not-Charming, collecting as much of it as she could under her fingernails. A staggered breath emanated from the bottom of her ribs. She was sure this dust was different. She leaned over it, resting her weight on her shins and curling her spine to bring her face close to the ground. She clenched her eyes shut, let out another shaky breath, and gasped for the thick, lovelier air. Lilith sobbed, guttural noises rising from the back of her throat. Her ribcage was wracked with each sound, and she pulled her lips back over her teeth, baring them slightly. She was not sure who the tears were for. Perhaps for her mother who would wake up tomorrow alone with her father. Or for herself, the daughter of the man who needed a son. Perhaps for the dying lights of Charming.

Digging her hands into the ground, Lilith collected handfuls of the foreign dirt and stood. She turned once again to face the town, her face stained, knuckles clenched white over the dirt, and mouth in a snarl. She waited for the wind to come and then with one last sob, threw the dust towards her town, hoping it would reach the window of her father and that he would know this was not the dust of Charming. That he would smell her own scent mixed with that of the dust and know that she no longer belonged to him.

Satisfied with the gesture, she sighed and brought her dirty hands up to wipe her face. A Mexican free-tail flew by, and the small breeze from its wings seemed to kiss her face. She did not think one had come that close since she was a child. She stooped to pick up the small satchel that held her spare dress and the biscuits she would eat tomorrow morning when she reached the smoky city beyond the thicket. Lilith stepped forward, without pausing this time, across the border and into the trees. Behind her, the last light of Charming flickered out.

Pain au Chocolat
Katie Cukrowski

The grass was irritating the sensitive skin on her bottom, so she slid onto the shawl beside her. She continued to talk to the two men confidently, more confidently than she would have been able to had she been wearing clothes. The weight of those petticoats, skirts, and hats on top of all the social rules constricted her. But to hell with sashes and societal conventions, she thought. If I want to picnic in the buff, I'll do it—and I'll do it proudly.

Looking again at the canvas, Chloé couldn't help but imagine what the woman must be thinking. Neither the woman's face nor her body was especially stunning, yet her self-assured expression and posture made her one of the most beautiful women Chloé had ever laid eyes on. More of Edouard Manet's paintings surrounded her, on the gallery walls, inviting other people to understand their beauty. His brush strokes, figure compositions, and bold color choices drew her in, and for a few minutes, Chloé became a part of that world. She was sitting in the grass with them too, eating a handful of grapes while they discussed the nature of truth. Although she was at work, an employee for the Musée d'Orsay, Chloé lived inside the paintings she was paid to watch and protect.

Meanwhile, the tourists who hurried from room to room of the museum talked loudly, barely glancing at the walls before returning to their blather. Chloé saw perfect people coming to life on the canvases. Yet, to her, few people ever stopped talking long enough to get a glimpse into the perfect worlds around them.

* * *

On her way home on the metro, she called Marc to ask if she could come over. His stop was only one before hers at La Courneuve Aubervilliers. When she arrived at his apartment building, a modern-looking, five-story structure, she buzzed number 314 on the pad.

"Yeah, Chloé, is that you?"

"Let me in. It's cold."

His apartment door was already propped open when she reached the top of the stairs.

"How was work today?" Marc asked, smiling when Chloé walked in the room.

"Long," she replied, throwing herself down on the couch dramatically.

When she sat up, a good-looking man stood before her. Light, wavy strands of hair fell on either side of his face down to his jaw line, the rest of his hair pulled into a tiny knot on the back of his head. Thick facial hair, though it was meant to look unkempt and free, showed evidence of manicuring above the lip line and in front of his ears. Square-rimmed glasses framed his eyes, and he either didn't have any eyelashes or they were too short and light to be seen. Corduroy pants rolled up to the ankle and a thin African print tee created a carefree, artistic look. One glance at his apartment told a different story, though; high, whitewashed ceilings and a view overlooking the conservatory grounds indicated that he had money. Sometimes, when the windows were open, Marc and Chloé could hear the symphony practicing in the afternoons.

Marc was a graphic designer, freelancing for a couple of marketing companies in the area. He specialized in eye-catching product packaging and insidiously simple logos. Over the last two years, Marc's designs had received a reputation for increasing a product's sales by over fifty percent, and companies compensated him well for his work.

Chloé went to the kitchen and uncorked a bottle of Côtes de Provence from the fridge and poured a full glass for both of them. Within minutes, Chloé's cheeks began to feel flushed; she had eaten only a small slice of Brie and three crackers all day. Settling in even more comfortably into the couch, she leaned her head back, enjoying the swirling fog in her head as it made its way throughout her body.

Before long, Chloé led Marc to his bedroom. She always enjoyed the first few minutes when she could see how much Marc desired her. Her pleasure mounted as he kissed and touched her hungrily, but before he could undress her, she got up to switch off the lights.

"Please can we keep the light on?" Mark pleaded with her like he did every time. "I like to see your body when we're together."

"No, I don't look good today."

"That's not true. You're the sexiest woman I know. Every part of you is beautiful."

"Not today," she replied. "I'm ovulating; it makes me feel so bloated." Chloé hadn't actually had a period in five weeks. "Besides," she said, "I ate a big dinner before coming over. It makes my stomach stick out."

"*Ma petite chou*, we have nothing to hide from each other," Marc said sitting on the bed. "See," he noted, looking down unabashedly at his nakedness.

"Next time," Chloé replied. "I'll be ready next time." Already, she was thinking of excuses to use for their subsequent encounters. It wasn't that Chloé actually thought she was fat; rather, she felt as though there were some standard, some level of potential that just hadn't been met yet. She could always be better.

When she was ready to leave, Chloé grabbed her leather cross-body bag to check the contents to make sure she had her phone, wallet, and keys. After making certain that she had everything, and while she waited for Marc to finish in the bathroom, she walked over to the door. When Marc saw that she was about to leave, he grabbed his own set of keys, so that he could walk her to the metro station. He didn't like her to walk by herself in the dark.

Chloé asked Marc what his plans were for the rest of the evening and Thursday. Aside from a design for the new packaging for *La Vache Qui Rit* that needed to be completed and sent out, he would be free by Friday night. They made plans to spend that evening together.

Under the naked light bulb at the top of the stairs leading down to the metro, they said their goodbyes. He kissed her softly, open mouthed, and she returned the kiss with a series of small dry pecks.

She sat alone on the red plastic seat, while the train sped and bumped along. Six minutes later, the train came to a stop at *Le Bourget*.

As she exited the metro station, she could see her apartment building peeking over the top of the *bureau de poste*. Five years ago, she had been fortunate enough to find a small studio apartment she could afford located in a fairly safe, residential neighborhood.

Her flat, despite its small size, felt open and roomy. Chloé had gone to a lot of trouble to section off the room as best as possible. Area rugs had been carefully placed on the floor, one for each of the living spaces. A dusty rose-colored piece of carpet peeked out from beneath her stylishly-made bed. A gift from her aunt and uncle for her twenty-eighth birthday last year, her duvet was simple and white, with tight Celtic knots woven throughout in a soft grey thread. It was not the kind of thing she would have picked out for herself, but Chloé loved how orderly and clean it always looked. At the foot of the bed, a tall wardrobe held every article of clothing she owned—except for her shoes, which were stored on tiny racks beneath the bed.

A smaller rug was snuggled up in the corner under a high-backed wooden chair. The chair was upholstered in a light brown linen fabric, complementing the wood stain. A metallic floor lamp had been placed beside the chair to create a cozy reading area. The kitchenette was off to the left of her bedroom and came equipped with an oven/stove unit, a microwave, sink, and refrigerator. And even though there was room for one, she didn't have a dining table.

Art prints that she bought for forty percent off in the gift shop were tacked up on all the available wall space above and beside her bed. Her favorite, another of Manet's works, hung in the center. Olympia, the porcelain-skinned courtesan, lay confidently on the bed, unashamed of her bare body. To Chloé, *this* was the ideal: to be poised, certain of who she was, assured of herself.

When Chloé walked inside, she took off her wool jacket and hung it with her purse on the coat rack behind the door. After being with a man, she always bathed as soon afterwards as she could. Chloé pulled off her riding boots and walked into the bathroom. While she disrobed, she turned on the taps to let the water heat up because it took nearly two minutes for the heater to get going. Steam was filling the room as Chloé stepped into the tub and lowered herself into the hot, shallow water. She inhaled the thick, humid air in deep, relaxing breaths as she sank into the water. Chloé always bathed because she perceived showers as yet one more manifestation of the fast-paced, in-and-out, temporary nature of modern society—a society unable to bask in true beauty, even for a moment.

As she reached for her sea salt scrub, Chloé thought about Marc, the way he touched her so tenderly. Grabbing handful after handful of the thick grainy oil, she exfoliated the surface of her skin, using the tips of her fingers to rub small circles, growing bigger and bigger until her flesh was nearly raw. Chloé had decided years ago in university that pink skin meant clean skin. After a quick washing of her long, dark brown hair, Chloé rinsed off and drained the tub.

Yet instead of grabbing a towel to dry off with, Chloé stood on the fuzzy bath mat, beads of water rolling down her body, quickly soaking the carpet fibers. Directly in front of her, on the back of her bathroom door, hung a full-length mirror.

Chloé sighed as she looked at the naked body reflected back at her. Yes, she was glad Marc hadn't seen her tonight.

Looking down at her thighs, she pinched the inside skin in her fists and decided that she would need to lose about a kilogram to keep her thighs from touching at the top. She slouched, and her previously flat stomach folded over, causing a line to appear just over her belly button. With a sigh, she straightened her posture. Her body was all wrong. It looked self-indulgent, not relaxed, sensual, alluring. "That's got to go," she said to herself. Chloé used to do vigorous core workouts and abdominal exercises to try to tone up her belly, but she never saw the kind of results she wanted. What she needed to do now was get her diet under control, reduce portions, and cut out sweets completely.

And then there were her breasts. Once so perky and firm, they seemed to be getting smaller and droopier. She cupped the flesh in her hands and lifted her breasts to an unrealistic height, giving her the kind of cleavage only attainable with an exceptionally supportive push-up bra. She dropped her arms to her sides.

In the back of her mind, Chloé knew she was beautiful; men had always given her attention and complimented her appearance, and her girlfriends expressed how they envied Chloé's slender frame, thick brown hair, and deep dimples in her cheeks. However, no voice was powerful enough to be heard over the one inside her own mind.

The wet strands of hair continued dripping water, keeping Chloé from ever getting dry. She shivered at last, turned away from the mirror, and pulled out a dry towel from the cabinet beneath the sink. Chloé walked over to her wardrobe and got out her nightclothes. Her favorite feeling was the sensation of putting a fresh pair of panties on after bathing, when the cool cotton is still tight from the wash.

As she slipped under the duvet and sank into the mattress, Chloé realized how exhausted her body was. She didn't even pick up the copy of *Aline et Valcour* from beside her bed, waiting until another day to finish the story of the lovers on the island of Tamoé.

At nine o'clock, her alarm went off. Chloé tried to open her eyes, but before she was able to, pain shot through her temples when she tried to lift her head. Chloé lay back down on the pillow, and slowly managed to ease herself into a sitting position in bed. Fifteen minutes later, she was able to stand and make a cup of green tea with lemon. The tea helped take the dizziness away, but more than anything, Chloé was hungry. Yet if she was going to stick with her resolution and lose the last three or four kilos, she could eat none of the food in her pantry. But Chloé did need to eat something before she felt sick again, especially before going to work that afternoon.

She tossed on her coat, pulled on a pair of boots, and threw a red scarf around her neck as she walked out the door. Just a block away was the small grocery stand, *Frais*. She decided that she would get a stalk or two of celery, a bundle of carrots, and a head of lettuce—if it looked fresh today. Ten minutes later, for just over two euros, Chloé walked away with a sack full of calorie-free options. But as she walked back home, making the full circle around the block, she smelled Paul's Patisserie.

"Damn!" she muttered. She had forgotten that she could not walk back this way without passing her favorite bakery. Chloé hadn't let herself go in for weeks because when she did go inside, she couldn't resist buying fresh *pain au chocolat*, hot baguettes, almond croissants, fruit tarts, and *mille feuille*.

Chloé looked at her bag of raw vegetables and then sniffed the air again. Her stomach turned over itself as the promise of rich, warm flavors seemed just within reach. She walked inside the bakery.

When she got home and laid out the spoils of her trip on the counter, she was giddy with excitement. Not only did she know how absolutely delicious each bite would taste, but the pastries themselves were a delight to look at. The bright slices of fruit on top of the tarts, the golden bread crusts, and the chocolate drizzle over the cakes called to Chloé.

Chloé picked up the warm *pain au chocolat* and brought it to her lips, readying herself for the indulgence. The buttery crust flaked off into a hundred pieces in her mouth, and as she chewed, the second flavor emerged—the chocolate center. Chloé smiled.

She spat the mouthful out into the trash. And then she took another bite of the pastry, chewing and spitting until the entire thing was an unrecognizable lump in the trashcan.

* * *

Even though Chloé knew she was not allowed to lean on the walls, today she decided that she didn't care. The soles of her feet ached from standing for the last six hours, and there was no one in her section of the gallery this near to closing time. The throbbing in her head was coming back as the ibuprofen wore off. Nonetheless, Chloé never second-guessed whether or not the pain was worth it.

In the canvas on Chloé's left, holding her yellow parasol, Claude Monet's faceless beauty stood in the grass, wind blowing from behind her. Chloé was so fascinated by this painting because every time she looked at it, she interpreted the woman's expression differently. Sometimes the woman looked peaceful and contemplative, but other times she looked lonely; sometimes she seemed sorrowful; most often though, she looked trapped. Images of beautiful women surrounded her, and Chloé studied every canvas with an eerie scrutiny that, Marc had once confided to her, made people feel uneasy when they saw her staring.

Every day, Chloé thought she looked more and more like the kind of woman the Impressionists would have wanted to paint—forever young, always poised and elegant. To Chloé, the way people lived now was simply grotesque. Women walked around the museum in dirty sneakers, pants too tight for them, with hair that hung limply above their shoulders. And the men were just as bad. Chloé once told Marc, "There simply isn't a gentleman in the bunch." With their untucked shirts and polyester backpacks swung over their shoulders, Chloé had actually recoiled once when a particularly disheveled man walked past her in the museum.

She thought that maybe she would meet an artist, a man who wanted to paint *her*. But not just anyone would have the honor. He would have to understand the sensitivities of women; paint them confidently—but not harshly. Each brush stroke would be powerful, yet soft. Of course, Degas, Courbet, Gérôme, Renoir, Manet, and Monet, they all knew how to treat a lady. They could encapsulate what it meant to be feminine,

47

beautiful, and alive within the confines of a one-meter by two-meter frame.

Chloé knew exactly what the painting of her would look like, but she also knew that she herself did not yet look like the woman in her fantasy. She decided that she needed a few more weeks before she would feel confident in her appearance. Then again, Chloé could not wait too long or her already aging body would only keep looking older and lose its youthfulness, something she could never get back. Many of the women in the paintings Chloé loved were not especially thin, nor did they all have attractive features, but they had bold confidence that Chloé both envied and found intoxicating.

Right after Chloé saw the last person leave her section, she felt someone behind her.

"Uh, it's Chloé, right?" asked a small voice as Chloé spun around quickly.

It was Colette, the new intern for the curating department. Easily a head shorter than Chloé, she reminded Chloé of a little fairy. Colette's short pixie hair, slight frame, soft voice, and easy smile all added to the effect.

"Uh-huh. You're Colette."

"It sure is empty up here. Aren't you ever bored when you're stuck all by yourself?" Colette looked sympathetically right into Chloé's eyes.

"No, I'm not. This is my home. All around me are wonderful people."

"Oh, so you get to talk to people when they're passing through and tell them about the art?"

"No, that's not who I talk to."

"Oh," Colette responded awkwardly. "Well, I just wanted to ask you if you'd like to go out with some of us when we get done here. We're going to *Satisfaire* for a bite to eat and drinks. We'd love for you to come."

Chloé had seen the people downstairs before and knew immediately that she had no intention of ever spending time with them. She scrambled for an excuse and decided on using her favorite one, a reason so incredibly vague that it was never questioned.

"Thank you for asking, but I can't. I have other plans tonight."

"Okay, well maybe next time, right?"

"Right."

Colette seemed satisfied with that, and with a beaming smile, she quickly turned her head and flitted out of the room.

Chloé sat down on the bench behind her, trying to remember what she had been thinking about before she was interrupted. Again, she wondered about posing for an artist and how he might paint her.

In *her* painting, Chloé lies on the bank of a river. She is wearing a clean, white frock, her left shoulder exposed because the sleeve has fallen down. Her hair is pinned up in hundreds of tiny ringlets, braided together on the crown of her head. Beside her is a woven hat laced with blue ribbon. A canopy of trees frames the top and sides of the painting, and Chloé rests on a bed of clovers, propped up slightly by the trunk of a tree. A beautiful face with dainty features and flawless skin, with just a touch of color on her cheeks, she looks directly out at the viewer. Her expression is bold. Chloé is perfect, but she is utterly alone. Everyone else stands together on the other side of the water.

The Continuing Controversy of The Snuggle Shack
Joe Dornich

Lonnie calls and tells me my first session isn't until noon, which is great because it means the protestors will be on their lunch break and not there to remind me that I'm a hell-bound gigolo. And a murderer. Of course, when I get to work there is a woman who has apparently brown-bagged it. She is perched on the curb with her protest sign across her lap, slowly destroying what appears to be an egg salad sandwich. She must spot my Snuggle Shack employee t-shirt, which advertises me as a "Certified Cuddler," because she bolts to attention, holding her sign high and proud. In bold, red letters, it reads: SNUGGLE SLUTS GO HOME! I want to ask this woman if she really thinks this is where I want to be. If she truly believes this is the life I always imagined for myself. But I don't. I just smile weakly and compliment her use of alliteration.

Across the street I see a giant hulk of a man, like an armoire with limbs. He's balding on the sides, and all the way bald up top, and the midday sun glints off of his huge, smooth dome. At first I think he's just another protestor, but he isn't holding a sign, or telling me what a terrible person I am. He just stares. He stares right at me. Then, the woman beside me starts screaming something about how I'm unraveling the fabric of this great and noble country, but it's hard to make out because her mouth is full of egg salad. I ignore them both and go inside.

Upstairs I find Lonnie in his office meditating beneath his eight watercolors of the Dalai Lama and the photo of himself and Stanley Geegland. Stanley is Lonnie's friend from rehab who bares an uncanny resemblance to Bono. He even wears the little rose-colored glasses. Mindy and Allison, our two female snugglers, are in awe of the photo, and while Lonnie never outright says it's Bono, he doesn't correct them either. If Lonnie is aware of my presence, he doesn't acknowledge it. I knock on the door jam, interrupting what I'm sure is his inevitable Transcendence Into

Enlightenment. Lonnie opens his eyes. He asks if my time away was mentally and spiritually recuperative. He asks if I am prepared to continue doing the healing work of Touch Therapy.

I say sure to both.

"I certainly hope so," Lonnie says. "The file is on the desk." Then he closes his eyes and continues his pursuit of Zen.

My first client of the day is one Sara Mews. According to her Snuggle Scenario we'll spend an hour in the Etruscan Room, on the bed, but above the covers. She has opted out of the Ambient Aural Therapy, which is great because that includes the Maui Waterfalls Fountain. That thing always makes me have to pee. Her file tells me that Sara suffers from social anxiety and mild depression. Her intake photo shows a thin, middle-aged woman who looks like she's never smiled in her life. I've seen mug shots with more glee. Even so, she's my first client since the incident, and I can't afford another suspension. Under her Preferred Therapy Postures, Sara has said that she'd like to start as the Little Spoon but is open to some possible Face-to-Face. So that's how we begin.

Though Lonnie officially runs The Snuggle Shack, his dad is bankrolling it. Mr. Johnson made his fortune inventing that white, foam tray beef is sold on. I guess before then meat was just wrapped in butcher paper, and the blood and other juices would leak out. Johnson's Meat Trays absorb those carnivorous reminders, and now they're in every deli and supermarket in the country. Mindy, Allison, and I call him the Meat Diaper Man, though never in front of Lonnie.

The story is that a few years ago Lonnie was living with a vet tech, and at some point became addicted to Canine Oxycodone. He did a few failed stints in rehab, but the last one had more of a holistic, mind-body type of intervention. Lots of touch therapy and elephant gods. Whatever it was, it worked, and Lonnie's been gulping the Energy Exchange Kool-Aid ever since. He promised dad he'd stay clean if, in return, he'd help turn his new interests into a business. Lonnie used the money to convert the offices of a defunct law firm into three Snuggle Suites, each with a couch, pillow-top bed, adjustable lighting, and those ambient nature CDs. Though we've only been open a few months, and some people are coming around to the idea of Contact Medicine, most of the town thinks we're running some kind of new-age brothel.

My session with Sara does not go well. During Big/Little Spoon my arm keeps falling asleep, and strands of her hair drift into my mouth. I sneeze an unacceptable number of times. Though she remains stoically silent, I can tell Sara would be more relaxed if she were being buried alive. I suggest we try some Face-to-Face. This is a mistake. Snuggle Protocol requires that Face-to-Face include prolonged periods of therapeutic stroking along the shoulders and back area. Normally this is fine, but Sara has a number of pronounced moles on her back, like God, or Jesus, or whoever, super-glued a handful of Raisinetes back there before forcing her into this world. Every time I begin one of my stroking maneuvers, I run up against one of Sara's moles and stop short. I'm afraid of accidently lopping one off. Instead, I resort to a series of tentative, gentle pats that probably have little therapeutic value. It's like frisking a baby. Sara's disappointment is profound. Her mouth curls down, deepening already prominent frown lines. Her eyes stare at me with the lidless disinterest of a reptile. It doesn't help that our faces are about six inches apart. My Snuggle Summary Evaluation does not look promising.

It doesn't take long. I'm sanitizing the slippers with disinfectant spray when Allison tells me Lonnie wants to see me in his office.

He's still in the lotus position when I arrive.

"Take a seat, please," he says.

There are no chairs in Lonnie's office, just a bunch of meditation pillows and a few yoga mats. I move to sit on a purple and gold cushion, but Lonnie says no. He means I should sit on the floor. So that's where I sit.

"I, we, all of us here are in the business of healing," he says. "And while of course the healing is our main objective, we depend on the business component to provide this service. The lights don't run on love, do they? I can't pay the rent on this place with smiles, can I?"

I admit that he cannot.

"So, until we all live in some kind of utopia where love and smiles are the primary means of commerce, we need the business. And that means clients. But you, you are driving those clients away from here, and in one case, right out of existence. At least, on this plane anyway."

Lonnie's talking about the woman I killed. Mrs. Dorothy Simone. Technically, she died of "natural causes," but that's a detail a number of people seem to be ignoring. Like the protestors. Like Lonnie.

"Each of us," he continues, "is striving for spiritual completeness, to find that harmonious balance between ourselves and our surroundings. We do this even though we know the journey will never end. Even though we know we will never be completely whole. Perhaps I've overestimated your position on this journey. Maybe, given your current level of wholeness, being a healing influence on others is asking too much. Does this make sense?"

I nod. I nod and try to ignore the fact that I'm having my "wholeness" judged by a guy who was once addicted to doggie smack.

"However," Lonnie says. "Despite the unfortunate scene with Mrs. Simone, she did like you. As do the rest of our advanced clientele."

He means old people.

"So, until further notice, they will make up your client list. I will handle everyone else, as well as any walk-ins. Mindy and Allison, per usual, will take care of our male clientele."

"And when I'm not embracing the elderly," I say. "Then what? What about the rest of my shift?"

"Equally divided between Maintenance and Housekeeping."

"C'mon Lonnie, you know I can't afford to change sheets all day. I need the tips."

"Then allow me to give you the most valuable tip of all," he says. "Unburden yourself from this negativity that is blocking your spiritual growth. Develop a calming, peaceful center, and allow it to expand and radiate out to others. Because, if you can't, you'll never know true serenity. Plus, I'll fire you."

Then Lonnie dismisses me, but not before giving me a copy of my Written Warning, which highlights the changes to my shifts. Lonnie's signed the bottom, and I notice he's dotted the i with a tiny yin and yang symbol.

A little piece inside of me dies.

I go back to work.

Mrs. Dorothy Simone was my regular nine-thirty Thursdays. She was a sweet old lady, though a bit eccentric. Always showed up for our session with her face completely made up, wearing full jewelry and some sequined ball gown like she was off to celebrate the repeal of Prohibition. I'd remind Mrs. Simone that we couldn't snuggle with her dressed like that, and she'd bring a manicured hand to an overly rouged cheek, and feign embarrassment. *You know,* she'd say, *if you want me to slip into something more comfortable, all you have to do is ask.* Then she'd call me "troublesome." Then I'd give her a pair of the pajamas we keep on hand for the lawyers and businesspeople who come in on their lunch breaks and don't want to wrinkle their suits.

We went through this routine every Thursday.

The day it happened, Mrs. Simone and I were snuggling on the couch in the Stillwater Room as usual, and after some time she put her head in my lap, and I ran a brush through her sparse, pewter-colored hair. She fell asleep, leaving a drool stain on my pants that looked like an upside down South America. I didn't mind. When our session ended, I tried to gently shake Mrs. Simone awake. Then I used a little more force. Still, I got no response. Of course Lonnie freaked, though, to me, slipping away in a painless, peaceful slumber seems like the utmost degree of relaxation, and something of a testament to my abilities as a Snuggler. Few saw it that way. Mindy wrote "The Cuddling Kevorkian" on my locker in red lipstick. Lonnie had to call for a Shutdown and bribe the EMTs to take Mrs. Simone's body out the back. Even so, the protestors got wind of it, and now they have a whole other reason to hate us. We all got sent home early, which meant lost revenue, and more than a few unpleasant looks in my direction. Did anyone ask if I was okay, if I suffered any residual trauma from having a woman die in my lap? They did not. Was I praised for not mentioning the fact I wouldn't be receiving my usual twenty percent tip? I was not. What I did get was three days Reflective Suspension. I thought about quitting. Then I thought about the shameful six months of trying to shop around my degree in Television History, and the realization that I am unqualified for just about every job out there.

I'm in Laundry, trying to wrestle the duvets back into the duvet covers, when Lonnie sticks his head in and says, "Phone." It's Gloria, the live-in I hired for Gramps. She says we have a problem. She says I need to come home right away. In the background I hear Gramps screaming that he's going to be late. Something made of glass breaks. I tell Gloria I'll be right there.

"I have an emergency at home," I say to Lonnie. "But I'll be back as soon as I can." He reminds me to breathe and focus on my bliss.

Outside, the protestors have returned from lunch en masse. When they spot me, their faces screw up in identical grimaces of judgment. They shout and shake their signs—DOWN WITH COMPANION$HIP, A-LONE IS BETTER THAN A-JOHN—in my face, as if hoping to fling their righteous wisdom on me.

Across the street is the balding armoire man from earlier. His body goes rigid when he sees me, and his face mottles like ground beef. He moves to cross the street, ignoring or oblivious to the cars that have to stop short to keep from slamming into him. Just as he's about to reach me, a man steps between us. He says that I, and the work I do, are affronts to the Lord. His tongue darts in and out of his mouth when he speaks, and flecks of spittle land on my shirt. He holds a sign with a Bible verse written on it, and though I don't know it specifically, I imagine it refers to my wayward soul, and the eternal hell-fires that will eventually consume it. Or something like that. The man says that I need to atone for my sinful ways and accept Christ into my life, just as he has. Then he bops me on the head with the cardboard end of his sign.

I rush home.

When I arrive, I find Gloria chasing Gramps around the loveseat. Gramps is wearing his navy blue pinstripe. Gloria looks more flustered than usual.

"I'm going to be late," Gramps says when he sees me. "This... woman here is making me very late."

On the floor, shattered into a dozen pieces, is one of mom's Adorable Occasions figurines. It is—was—a calf and a tiger cub on a teeter-totter. I never liked that one. It never made sense to me, biologically speaking. Sure, maybe their friendship works for a while because they're young and don't know any better. But once that tiger cub grows up and realizes where he fits in this world, and what's expected of him, he's going to pounce off that teeter-totter and turn that calf into veal and wallets.

"What are you going to be late for?" I ask Gramps.

"Work, of course. I have to be at the office by nine."

"No," I say. "You don't. You don't have to work anymore. You're retired."

Gramps looks around the room and then at Gloria and me as if we've invaded his dreams. "I am?" he says.

"Yeah," I say. I take Gramps by the arm and lead him to his bedroom. His hands are trembling, and I help him remove his suit jacket and loosen his tie. It's amazing. Most of the time the poor guy has no idea where he is, or what's going on, but he can still tie the cleanest Half-Windsor I've ever seen. It's like he's here just long enough to realize how fast he's going.

"This is not working," Gloria says as she sweeps up porcelain animal pieces.

"I know," I say. "And I'm sorry. I know he's been challenging lately, but there's a new medication, and maybe..."

"No, not just the Señor," Gloria says. "You and I. I have not been paid in three weeks. I cannot afford."

"Please. Just give me a few more days. Here," I say as I pull out my wallet, immediately and painfully aware of the futility of this gesture. I open it, hoping I guess that the pair of dollar bills inside have mated and reproduced. No such luck.

"Take this," I tell her. "I'll have some more for you soon."

But Gloria just stares at my meager offering and smiles. She spends more on the bus coming out here.

"I'm sorry," she says. "I cannot." Then she hands me the broom, grabs her purse, and walks out.

I stand at the window, hoping Gloria will change her mind, or at least glance back at us one more time. She does neither. Gloria becomes, along with Sara Mews, the second woman today to walk out on me filled with disappointment.

I'm on a roll.

I microwave some hotdogs for dinner, and Gramps and I settle in to watch his favorite show, *Pre-K MMA*. We're just in time for the main event. The announcer says today's bout features the toughest tots this side of the Mississippi: "Tiger" Timmy Witherspoon versus Preston "The Blade" Dempsey. The Tiger looks big for his age. Gramps suspects him of doping. The fight is less mixed martial arts, and more of an arms flailing, windmill type of exchange. The Blade has some good moves, but his head is too big for his body, and it keeps throwing him off balance. A couple of times the Tiger wanders off in the wrong direction, and the ref has to reset.

"Your mother came to visit me last night," Gramps says in between bites of hotdog.

This is an impressive bit of news as mom's been dead almost a year now.

"Really?" I say. "How's she look?"

"She's worried about you. She thinks you spend too much time alone. She wants you to meet a nice girl."

"Well," I say. "If you two somehow talk again, tell her I'm fine. Tell her I'm not lonely. I meet nice girls every day."

We watch the rest of the fight. In the third round The Blade trips on his own feet and bites his tongue. He cries on the mat until the ref counts him down, and the Tiger wins by Technical Knockout, and that's that.

I'm back at work on Tuesday, which is when the van arrives from Renaissance Gardens. The RG is a top-tier assisted living facility. I'd love to move Gramps there, but that place takes some serious bucks. I can't even afford the warped linoleum and wet bacon smells of Wavering Meadows. The protestors are pretty well behaved on Tuesdays, as most people are usually reluctant to yell at the elderly. Sure, some people still shake their signs and chant how "Hugs Beget Whoredom," but most find it tough to sling their condemnation at someone's Bubby while she hobbles past in her pink housecoat.

I've brought Gramps to The Shack with me. It seemed like the best way to keep him out of trouble. Allison says she'll help keep an eye on him and maybe work in a free Snuggle Session if there's time. Allison is great. She's my girl, or she would be if she only realized how much we had in common. Her dad left too, walking out on her and her mother and brother when Allison was just a teenager. I guess her mother couldn't cope because at the end of October that same year she hung herself from the oak tree in their front yard. Allison's little brother was the first to find her. He was too small to get her down, and none of the neighbors intervened because they thought she was an elaborate Halloween decoration. By the time Allison got home, her brother was sitting in the grass with his knees to his chest, rocking back and forth in the shadow of his mother. He's been in and out of the nut-hut ever since.

I want to take Allison out, maybe down to Cooler's Pub. We'd talk about our respective situations. How, because of her brother, and me with Gramps, we both know what it's like to sacrifice for a loved one, how we'd do anything for them, but sometimes, usually late at night, the thought of that responsibility sits like a weight on our chest, and it's hard to breathe. And even though helping them likely amounts to the one decent thing in our lives, it also fills us with a paralyzing sense of remorse, not to mention the crippling debt. Then, maybe after all of that, we'd share a plate of potato skins.

But I don't. I don't ask Allison out. I'm too shy I guess, or afraid she'll say no. Plus, I think she likes Lonnie.

The ladies from Renaissance Gardens keep me busy all morning. One client talks about her late husband, a tugboat captain, as she rests her head on my chest. She says her hands and fingers have become so thin she's had to move her wedding ring to her thumb, and since then nothing has felt the same. Another talks about how some of the women at the home cheat at Bridge. She insists on being the Big Spoon, and every time she recounts a lost hand, she gives me an angry little squeeze. Someone's grandma, who smells like buttered toast, spends the hour telling me about the time she was propositioned by Spiro Agnew in the elevator of a Baltimore Howard Johnson's.

Things slow down in the afternoon, and Lonnie decides I should use the free time to repaint one of the Snuggle Suites. Lonnie is always finding these weird paint colors that are supposed to have healing properties and evoke some kind of therapeutic something or other. The color he's picked for Suite 3 is called Shantung. Lonnie says it's the shade of the sun just as it rises. He says it's the color of new possibilities, of seeing things in a fresh light. I say it looks yellow to me, and Lonnie says that's exactly my problem. Then he presses some money into my hand and says four gallons ought to cover it.

I decide to take Gramps with me. I find him in the Stillwater Room, on the loveseat with Allison. His head is on her shoulder, and she is holding one of his hands in both of hers. They've got Rain on a Tin Roof playing as their Ambient Aural Therapy. I've always liked that one.

Allison must hear me come in because she looks up and smiles at me. A strand of her chestnut-colored hair falls across her face.

Oh, Allison. When will our time come? When will we—free from having to sweep up the little tumbleweeds of lint and hair that collect under the beds, or having to constantly restock the scented candles because they burn down so quick because Lonnie is too cheap to buy the good ones—have our moment? Some time where we can talk, and not just idle chitchat, but about grander, deeper topics. And maybe, during this conversation, one of us, say me, makes a comment that, while on the surface is witty, also speaks to a more profound, emotional understanding of things. And perhaps, in response to this witty/emotional comment, one of us, say her, laughs and gently touches my arm, letting her hand linger for just a second. When will that happen?

Allison catches me staring at her, and her eyes seem to brighten, as if lit from within.

Maybe now, I think. Maybe now is our moment. Then Gramps catches me staring.

"Who the hell is this guy?" he asks.

Maybe not.

"Hi, Gramps," I say. "You having a nice time?"

He turns to Allison. "Do you know this young man?" he asks.

Gramps always refers to me as a "young man" when he doesn't recognize me.

"Sure," Allison says. "He's your grandson."

Gramps stares at her, and then me, giving us the same blank look. Prerecorded rain continues to fall.

"I've got some errands to run," I say. "I think you should come with me."

Gramps starts making this low, humming noise, and slowly shaking his head.

"I'll take you to lunch," I say.

The humming stops, and his posture straightens. "Schotblatt's?" he asks.

That's just great. Gramps doesn't remember me, whom he has known my entire life, but he can recall, with immediate clarity, the Reuben from Schotblatt's Deli.

"Sure. Schotblatt's it is," I say, and off we go.

As Gramps and I exit The Shack, the protestors quiet down and step aside, creating a little path. I think finally I'm catching a break.

But no. The protestors aren't stepping aside for me. They're making room for the Bald Armoire. He stops a few feet in front of me. He's got a look of concentration on his face that makes the skin around his eyes crinkle.

59

"Was it you or the other guy that done it?" he says.

"Done what?" I say.

"Killed my mama."

Growing up, Mom always said that I had a smart mouth, that I didn't think before I spoke. She said that one day, my smart mouth would get me in trouble.

And she was right. Because instead of apologizing, or explaining what really happened, or offering any measure of sympathy, I say this: "Holy crap! Mrs. Simone was *your* mom? I never knew she had a son. In all the time we spent together, she never once mentioned you."

I know, as the words leave my mouth, that this is probably an ill-advised response. The Armoire winces. Then he does this ragged-type breathing through his nose that makes his massive chest rise and fall. Then, as if to confirm my suspicions, he pulls a gun from the waistband of his jean shorts and shoots me.

The Bald Armoire shoots me right in the stomach. I can't believe it. The impact knocks me right on my rear, which, oddly, hurts more than the bullet and fresh hole in my gut.

The gunshot creates a panic. The protestors flee in every direction, their abandoned signs littering the sidewalk. Even The Armoire seems to have disappeared. The peace and quiet is a welcomed change, even if it, I suppose, comes at a hefty price.

I lie back and stare at the sky. There are no clouds.

After some time I feel my shoulders and head rise, and I think this is it; my body is ascending to that vast and mysterious beyond just like movies and TV always promised. Then I'm disappointed that even death has become a cliché. Then I feel the scratch of polyester against my cheek and realize it's Gramps pulling me into his lap.

"There, there young man," he says as he gently pats me on the head. "Help will be along soon. Try to lie still."

And even though it hurts my neck, I tilt my head back to look at my grandfather. He looks down at me and smiles and continues to stroke my hair.

"You know," he says, "my grandson is taking me to lunch today."

I look away. I close my eyes.

You would think, that after so many times of Gramps forgetting who I am, that it wouldn't hurt anymore. But it still does.

It hurts every time.

Breathe
Theresa Ener

I open my eyes. I see the ceiling of my mother's guest bedroom. I close my eyes. Not the best way to wake up. Funny how I could forget where I am.

I lie on my mom's fold-out futon, my eyes closed tightly, waiting for the panic that I know is coming.

I can smell coffee. Mom must be up. And I smell eggs. Not a smell I can tolerate on a good day, and today it's even more nauseating. I like the *taste* of eggs—fried, scrambled, egg-in-the-hole (mom's specialty)—but the sulfurous smell reeks, stinking up the whole house. I know she means well, though, and the kids will probably appreciate a homemade breakfast.

Gabby's warm toddler body is snuggled close to me. She stirs a little and sighs in her sleep, just like she always has. I used to lie awake in bed at night, listening to the baby monitor, listening to her sleep.

I can't feel Michael in the bed with us, but he is there, probably pressed up against the wall, giving me space, maintaining distance. And I can hear his rhythmic breathing. I'd know that soft snore anywhere. He's twelve now, but a mother never forgets things like that. I saw helplessness in his eyes last night when he crawled into bed with me and Gabby. I didn't ask him to be with us. I wouldn't have dared, but he felt it was his duty, I guess, to be near, to be our protector.

I think some of this has to do with what his uncle said to him last night. I wish I'd been the one to speak to Michael first, to tell him in my own words, but I didn't get the chance. I couldn't do *anything*.

It hasn't even been a full day. Things can change so much in such a short period of time. No one expects tragedy. It just blows in, unannounced, and screws up everything. Like a mammoth tornado, an F5, destroying everything that "is." And here we are, left to pick up the pieces, to dig through the rubble, to find something recognizable, something we can cling to, something to carry us over.

I want to curl into myself, crawl into a corner, and let someone else clean up the mess. I'm here, and he isn't. Gabby and Michael need me, and I can't let them down. Other than that, I'm at a loss. Or as someone said while I wailed in grief, "Take it one day at a time. And when one day is too much, take it one moment at a time. You can do that. You *can*." How about one breath at a time? One breath seems doable right now.

When I open my eyes again, Meredith is peeking through a small crack in the door. She tells me that breakfast is ready and then insists that she will be going with me today, to make the arrangements.

Michael sits up, scoots to the end of the futon. He asks if I need anything, then leaves for breakfast.

The door closes, and I slowly exhale, as if I could rid myself of all this worry in one long release of air. In with the good, out with the bad

I nudge Gabby, trying to rouse her. "No 'wake, mama."

I brush the dark curls out of her face and kiss her on the forehead. "Gabby-girl, time to wake." I kiss both of her cheeks, her nose. "C'mon, Grumpy. Up, up, up."

Her eyelashes flutter, and she feigns a pout in mock protest. "Mean, mean, Mama," she sleepily giggles. It's our joke. She's Grumpy Gabby in the mornings, and I am Mean Mama. Some things *do* stay the same.

2

Haylee's arrival is announced by Gabby. "Lee-Lee! Lee-Lee!"

We've all missed her, Gabby especially. For the first few weeks after Haylee left for college, Gabby carried around one of Haylee's favorite sweatshirts. She never put that sweatshirt down, gripping it with a tiny iron fist, not even willing to give it up for a quick wash. I'd try to pry that Gators sweatshirt away from her, but she'd scrunch her chubby face in fierce determination and shake her head "no."

Maybe Haylee can help me find a way to get through to Gabby. Maybe Haylee can help both of us.

"Mom . . . Mom!"

"Geez, Haylee, I'm right here."

She grabs me and just about smothers me in a bear hug.

"Mom, I don't understand . . . why?"

Haylee sits there with her arms crossed, looking at me as though I might offer some sort of explanation.

"I don't understand either, Haylee. I don't know if we ever will. At least that's what everyone keeps telling me. Am I supposed to be okay with not knowing? Why do people say that? It makes me feel more confused and helpless."

"Why would he do this? Especially to Michael and Gabby? They don't deserve this."

"Yeah."

"I don't mean that you deserve it, Mom. That's not what I meant."

"I know."

She sighs and opens her mouth to speak but then pauses. She shakes her head like she's not sure what she wants to say, but then she blurts out, "Mom, I loved Mike and all, but I'm freakin' pissed! This is bullshit."

She's crying now. I feel like I should say something, but I can't find the words. I just sit there, fidgeting with the fringe on the throw pillow.

"I'm sorry, Mom. I'm not trying to make you feel bad. But I hate that he did this."

"I get it. Really. I'm feelin' it too. Pissed off, hurt, confused, sad, whatever."

The rest of the family is buzzing around in the background. Mom is attempting to whisper. She's telling my brother that someone needs to sit me down and give me "the details." But I don't want to know. It's probably some sort of denial, but I don't care. Denial works for me right now.

"Mom?"

"Sorry. I kinda zoned out."

"It's okay. I'm gonna go see if Gabby wants to go swimming with the other kids. Max and Kenzie are already in the pool, but Gabby wouldn't get in until I got here. Do you need anything? I can take her shopping later. She's gonna need something to wear, ya know? Or I can go home and see if she has something in her closet."

"I don't want you at the house. I don't want anyone at the house. I'm not ready."

3

Meredith and I barely speak the entire drive. Small talk feels awkward. If I open myself to casual chatter, sooner or later she'll find a way to talk about Mike, about us, and I'm not in the mood. Mer must've gotten the hint from my terse responses; we both withdraw into our thoughts.

I spend the rest of the twenty-minute ride staring out the window counting white cars—twenty-nine—and out-of-state plates—*Alabama, Louisiana, Florida.* I absentmindedly fiddle with my wedding band and ponder whether my outfit is appropriate for the occasion.

We turn into the circle drive, and my stomach churns. The building's exterior is nothing special, an ordinary brick façade masking the somber business carried out inside

Meredith parks the sedan, checks her hair in the rearview mirror, and applies Chapstick before opening her door. I sit waiting, staring out the windshield at the Dairy Queen across the street. A rusted Plymouth is idling noisily at the drive-thru menu board. A plume of exhaust billows out of the tailpipe; the driver seems to be arguing with the kid who is hanging out the rear passenger window. I can hear the squawk from the speaker: *Is that a large peanut butter cup Blizzard, ma'am? And did you want whipped cream on that strawberry sundae?*

Mr. Caldwell is on the veranda, waiting for us. His hands are clasped in front of him; his smile is barely perceptible, respectfully reserved. These guys weird me out, the unhurried way they move and speak, the way they carefully choose their words, scripted to comfort the bereaved. He reaches out to clasp my hand in both of his. His skin is smooth and cool. I stare at his impeccably-manicured nails, wondering if he frequents a nail salon.

Mr. Caldwell's voice pulls me out of my musing. "Mrs. Donovan, I hope you will accept my deepest condolences. I know how difficult this process can be. I will do my best to assist you and your family in this time of need."

We follow him into the entryway and down a long, dimly-lit hallway. The smell of flowers is making me gag. Carnations.

We pass an open chapel door where a placard displays the name of Mrs. Mildred Myers. I glimpse dozens of floral arrangements around the dearly departed. Apparently Millie's family is awfully generous, bestowing the final reward for living ninety-two years, a floral sendoff in a stuffy chapel with Kleenex boxes at the end of each pew.

Mr. Caldwell leads us into a seating area just outside his office. He motions toward the chairs, his arm sweeping the scene like a *Price Is Right* beauty showcasing a plaid living room set, complete with glass-topped tables and faux Persian rug. *I'll bid $2450, Bob!*

He leaves us there while he goes to get my "portfolio."

"Why are we sitting out here? Shouldn't we be conducting our business inside the office? Isn't that what offices are for? I'm not here for social hour."

"Sam, that's how they do things. He's a nice man, really. Don't get all bothered about everything."

"I'm not *bothered*. I just don't get it, that's all. I guess sitting on a cushy Broyhill chair is supposed to ease my discomfort. Fat chance."

I perch on the edge of the chair, my hands in my lap, fingers threaded. Mer is picking lint off her sweater. I can see the corner of her mouth twitching as she digs in her pocket for a peppermint and a tissue. She looks up to see me eyeing the tissue warily. She sighs and wanders off in search of a caffeine fix.

I rummage in my purse for the envelope Mike's boss dropped off this morning. The cheery company logo belies the contents. I unfold the letter and read it again.

The paper feels dry and cold. I stuff the letter into the crack of the chair, not wanting to touch it anymore. Life insurance. I hadn't known he had a policy. I wonder if he thought about the policy at the end. I wonder if he knew it would be paid. I wonder if he thought about anything at all.

When Mer returns, I'm staring at the ceiling hoping gravity will keep the inevitable tears from betraying my hardened exterior. She eases onto her chair, cradling her Styrofoam cup, and takes slurps of her coffee, oblivious to my irritated glances.

"I wonder how much longer this is going to take. I don't like leaving Gabby for too long."

"I'm sure Haylee is keeping her occupied."

"Mr. Caldwell needs to get on the ball."

As if summoned, he appears, wielding the long lost portfolio. "I really am sorry you had to wait."

"It's okay. We have all the time in the world. Mike isn't going anywhere, right?"

"Samantha! I'm so sorry, Mr. Caldwell. My sister is under a lot of stress right now."

"Oh, I understand. These things take a toll. I was informed that your husband's insurance policy was paid in full. I'm sure that is such a blessing to you and your family. We try to make the arrangements as affordable as possible, but the financial burden can be significant for those who are not prepared."

Mr. Caldwell fires off a list of *necessities*: a memorial in the local paper, a motorcycle policeman to lead the procession, a family car, an organist, a dozen or so copies of the death certificate.

"What?"

"Death certificates, Mrs. Donovan. You will need multiple copies to inform your creditors and such."

I stand abruptly, dislodging the letter from its hiding place. "Are we done with this part? Do you need me to sign something so we can move on?"

"I'll have you sign some paperwork when the arrangements have been completed."

"Okay, well, I'm going to the restroom."

In the restroom I lock myself in a stall and lean against the door, my forehead resting on the metal, its coolness soothing the beginnings of a headache. My eyes are closed, my rapid breathing and quickened heart gradually returning to normal. After a few minutes, I open the stall and splash water on my face. I look like shit; I feel like shit.

"Sam, you okay in there? Mr. Caldwell has another appointment in an hour."

I brush past Meredith and hurry back to the seating area.

"Ladies, shall we proceed?"

We are escorted into the showroom. I stand for a moment, breathing in the scent. It reminds me of my grandfather's woodshop. He made each of his daughters and granddaughters a hope chest where they could stash away dreams for a future happy marriage. I'd always kept spare linens in mine until Haylee hid in it one day and panicked when she couldn't open the lid. Mike installed a lock and used the chest for his coin collection and old Army keepsakes. And his pistol.

Trying to get a sense of what Mike would have wanted, I run my hands along the glossy woods: the striated oak; the smooth, blonde maple;

the deep, rich mahogany. Tufted satin pillow tops, hidden drawers for letters and mementos, gold and silver adornments crafted on corners. Mike never would have wanted any of this. I'm ready to opt for a pine box.

Mr. Caldwell is patient and helpful.

"Was Mr. Donovan a hunter? Or a fisherman? We have a very beautiful piece with a hand-stitched woodland scene. Or perhaps a peaceful lake? Those seem to be the favorites."

I almost expect him to spout stats about extended warranties and fuel efficiency. Perhaps he'll duck into the back room to "consult with his sales manager" and return with a heck of a deal I just can't walk away from.

"Mike wasn't the outdoorsy type. He did have a fondness for Nascar, though. Do you have anything with a checkered flag? That would be *great*."

Mr. Caldwell is speechless.

Meredith attempts to get negotiations back on track. "Sam, I'm sure there's something here that will suffice, something that fits Mike's personality."

"Just pick one. I need to step outside. Excuse me." I exit through the back door into the carport. A young Hispanic sitting on a metal foldout chair eyes me like I'm intruding. He's cleaning underneath his fingernails with a pearl-handled pocketknife, methodically scraping away grit and grime. I look for a place to retreat but see only another foldout chair leaning against the brick wall near Mr. Perturbed. I nod my head in the direction of the chair, hoping he gets the message so I won't have to speak. He shrugs, so I open the chair and place it a few feet from him.

He pulls a battered pack of Marlboro Reds out of his denim shirt pocket, tilting his head my way. *Yeah, I'll take one of those.* I haven't smoked since my senior year in high school. Mr. P. hands me his lighter—a Betty Boop pin-up girl number. Keeping it classy. The first drag catches me off guard, and I cough. He starts to chuckle, then stops himself.

"You can laugh."

"I don't want to show no disrespect. People get upset."

"I ain't those people."

P. just sits there, taking long drags on his cigarette, giving me my mental space. I close my eyes and try not to think. I focus on the faint sounds of P.'s inhaling and exhaling. My shoulders relax, and my head begins to clear. P. starts to hum a melody I don't quite recognize. I think it's a hymn, something about sheaves and weeping and rejoicing.

I listen to the hymn and watch the smoke waft and waver over our heads. I lean back against the brick wall, feeling the dampness of the brick seep into my hair. The cigarette and the melody calm me. I breathe in the nicotine, savoring every inhalation and exhalation, enjoying the buzz. When I finish my cigarette, I stub it on the concrete.

P. lights another off his first, tossing the burning stub onto the driveway. Before he puts the pack away, he holds it out to me.

"Nah, I'm trying to quit."

"Yeah, these things will kill ya."

He laughs. I smile.

4

When I walk in the back door, I hear Gabby's voice coming from the guest bedroom.

"No, Lee-Lee! He's home. He is!"

"He isn't, sweetie. I promise. Remember how, in the book, the daddy rabbit got really sick and went to live with Jesus? Remember, the daddy wasn't at home anymore with little rabbit."

"Stupid book! Stupid stupid!"

"Haylee, what's going on in here?" I set my purse down and scoop up Gabby. She clings to me, trembling. "You read the book to her already? I told you I was going to sit down with her tonight and read it."

"She kept asking about him! What was I supposed to do?"

Mom hears our raised voices and comes to take Gabby out of the room. "Hey, sweet girl, you want a popsicle? I bought the kind you like, the ones with the ice cream in the middle."

She carries Gabby out of the room, scolding me with her glare.

Haylee waits for Mom to leave before she lets me have it. "What the hell? Why are you upset with me? I only tried to help. Aunt Corinne and Gram were talking about Mike not being here for my graduation and all the other important events in our lives, and they didn't realize Gabby was playing behind the couch and overhead. She wanted to know where he is and why he won't be here. She kept asking, Mom. What was I supposed to do?" She sits on the bed, her shoulders sagging with the weight of this unwanted responsibility.

I sit next to her, unsure what to say, so I reach out to take her hand in mine. She looks at me with tears in her eyes.

"Mom, I'm sorry. I was only trying to help."

"You didn't do anything wrong, Haylee. I'm sorry for the way I reacted. Seeing Gabby upset kinda freaked me out."

"After we read the book, I really thought she understood. Then a little while later she came up to me and said it was time to go home because Daddy missed her. I tried to say the right things, Mom, but she's just too young. I didn't know what else to do."

Gabby and Mom walk past the guest room on their way outside. Gabby is explaining why purple popsicles are her favorite—they taste like grape Kool-Aid—and why green is her least favorite flavor—it tastes like medicine.

Haylee bites her lip and clears her throat.

"I'm not going back to school this semester. I'm staying home with you."

"Uh, no you're not! Haylee, I can't let you do that. You have four weeks left. No way am I letting you lose this semester."

"It's okay. I'll be back on track in the fall. It's no big deal."

Mer walks in, sets two coffee mugs on the bedside table, and walks out.

"Haylee, I don't want you to leave school. You've worked so hard this semester. I don't want you to lose those credits. I'll be okay, really. Mike wouldn't have wanted this. He was so proud of you."

"Well, then he should've stuck around. He doesn't get a vote." She picks up her coffee mug and leaves the room.

Yeah, he doesn't get a vote.

5

The rumble of thunder awakens me a little after daybreak. It's raining.

I listen to the rain pelt the windowpanes, counting the moments between the thunder and the flash of lightning. I watch the clock and count how many seconds I can hold my breath: *one Mississippi, two Mississippi...*

I hear everyone rushing around, trying to get ready.

I reluctantly get up, gather my things, and go in search of an empty bathroom so I can shower. When I pass by the kitchen, Mom sees me. "Samantha, you can use my shower. I kept it clear just for you. And I saved you some breakfast."

I step into the kitchen to plant a kiss on top of Gabby's head and grab a cup of coffee.

"I had pancakes, Mama, with the chocolate chips. Gram made a smiley face."

"Oh, that's pretty cool, Gabby girl. Gram used to do that for me when I was little."

"We made one for you, Mama!" She proudly points to a huge pancake with a lopsided chocolate chip grin.

"Thank you, sweet girl." I give her another kiss, and then head to the shower.

I turn the water to near scalding and stand under the stream, letting the heat wash away the tension. The small bathroom fills with steam. Even after I wipe the mirror, my reflection is still lost in a hazy film clinging to the glass. I turn on the exhaust fan to clear the air. I hum along with its rhythmic sound, repeating the same tune I had heard P. humming. I go about the business of prepping for this dreaded day. When I open the door, I realize the rain has stopped.

6

I sit on the front pew, wedged between Mom and Mer. They refuse to leave my side no matter how many times I tell them I'm perfectly fine by myself. I don't need babysitters. From where I'm sitting, I should have a clear view of Mike, but the steady flow of friends, family, coworkers, neighbors, church members, etc. creates an impenetrable wall between us. The two hour visitation passes in a sea of familiar and unfamiliar faces and voices, a blur of blacks, grays, and navies swimming before me, offering hugs, pats, mumbled offerings of bereavement. The chapel is warm and stuffy, making it hard for me to breathe. The overpowering scent of flowers makes my sinuses swell in protest. I can feel a headache building, a tightening band stretched across my forehead. My stomach grumbles, and I realize I forgot to eat my special pancake.

It seems like I've been sitting in this spot for days. How many people are going to pass through before Mr. Caldwell announces the end of visitation? And that music is getting on my last nerve. Who picked this stuff? Did I sign off on this? It was probably Mer.

At one point, someone—one of Mike's coworkers, I think—hands me a picture frame, saying something about Mike's desk. During a brief lull in the procession, I glance down at the frame. It's a picture of me, Mike, and the kids, taken last Christmas. I'd had it framed so he could take it to work. I wanted him to have a recent picture of all of us, to keep him focused during those days when he was struggling.

I stand up, walk toward him, open the memento drawer, and slide the picture inside. I don't even look at his face. I simply shut the drawer and turn to walk away. When I look up, I see that everyone is watching me, their pity-stricken faces waiting to see what I'll do next, waiting for me to break down into a sobbing mess. But I am a disappointment, a sad excuse for a grieving widow. I walk out of the chapel with my head held high and my mascara intact.

Mer rushes to catch up to me. "Sam, what's going on with you? You act like we're the enemy, like we've done something wrong."

"I want this to be over."

"Sam, I know you may not understand that, but some of us need this process. It's our way of honoring him and the man that he was."

"It's only making things worse for me. None of you understand *that.*"

"I'm sorry."

"I'm going to sit in the back room. I'd appreciate if all of you just left me alone until the service starts. Okay?"

"Sure, Sam. I'll tell everyone you need some space. I'll come get you in a little bit." She walks away with her head down, looking defeated.

7

After the service, we all go back to Mom's for food and fellowship. Gabby makes sure I eat my pancake. It's the only thing I'm able to eat the rest of the day. I've changed into jeans and a t-shirt and settled myself beside the pool. Mer brings me a stack of stamped, addressed, thank you cards: *Thank you for the beautiful flower arrangement. Thank you for the delicious casserole. Thank you thank you thank you.* All I have to do is sign my name. Even that feels like too much effort, but I oblige. *Thank you for taking care of Gabby and Michael. Thank you for helping with all of the arrangements. Thank you for giving me space when I needed it. Thank you for putting up with me.*

8

The first thing I notice is that Mike's truck isn't in the driveway. I wonder where it is. My brother probably parked it at his house. That seems like something he'd do.

The front porch is full of plants: lilies, ivies, and various potted plants that will be neglected. Mike had the green thumb. I couldn't even keep a fern alive. I'll dole out the plants to family, friends, neighbors, the mailman, perhaps.

I pause at the front door, key in hand. When I step inside I am assaulted by the smell of bleach. Mom told me the ladies from church had been over to clean: everything spotless; a trauma-free homecoming; nothing in sight to upset me. I guess that was their intention, but the chemical odor only reminds me of what was there before they came to clean. I can only imagine what they had to see. *Thank you for making our home inhabitable again. I'm sorry you had to see that. I'm so sorry.*

I walk around, making mental notes about what needs to be put away and what can stay out in the open, what will probably be donated to charity and what can be packed away to give to Gabby and Michael later, when they're older

I finally make my way to our bedroom. I stand in the doorway, staring at my hope chest, wondering how something that was created with love could have held something that destroyed a marriage, took away a father, a son, a brother, and a friend. I envision him putting the key in the lock, lifting the lid, pushing aside my grandmother's quilt, rummaging for the green metal box, hesitating before taking the .45 from its case, then walking to the bathroom. I hear his footsteps, slow and deliberate; I hear his shallow, measured breathing as he gathers the courage to do what he has determined is the only answer, the only way out. I walk over and place my hands on the closed door; I press my ear to the wood, listening, hoping to hear something, anything. There is nothing. I am left with nothing.

In the kitchen, I go to the corner cabinet and take out the familiar purple bag: his favorite whisky, our Friday whisky. *To the weekend*, we'd toast.

I grab two glasses and the whisky before going out on the porch to sit on the swing. I pour a glass for each of us. I breathe in the sweet smell. I take a sip; the slow burn is comforting, warming me, giving me strength. I take off my wedding band and hold it up, letting the sunlight reflect off the diamonds. I pick up the purple cloth bag and place the ring inside, my hand brushing something at the bottom of the bag. I pull out a piece of paper, folded into a two inch square, with my name written on the outside: *Sammy*. Only Mike called me Sammy.

I clutch the note tightly in my hand, the corners digging into my palm, the pain keeping me present. I feel my chest rising and falling with each nervous breath; I hear the blood rushing through my veins. Seconds pass and then minutes. I breathe. I wait.

I finish my drink and then Mike's. Calm envelopes me. I unscrew the lid of the whisky bottle and drop the ring inside. I watch it sink, hear the soft clink when it hits the bottom, and notice that it looks even more beautiful in the amber liquid. I take a deep breath and unfold the note. I read his message to me, again and again, staring at the paper, hoping to feel something. But I feel nothing. I roll up the note and drop it into the mouth of the bottle. I watch it float until it is saturated, sinking down into the whisky, unrolling, revealing the words he left to me, the words that cannot bring him back, the words that give me no solace, no answers.

I am sorry, Sammy. Please forgive me.

—M

I screw the lid on the bottle, place it inside the bag, and tie the gold string tightly in a bow. I carry it inside the house, open the cabinet door, and place the bag on the shelf. I push it as far into the cabinet as I can reach, all the way to the back where there is no light, where no one will see it, where it will be forgotten. Then I shut the cabinet door, take a deep breath, turn around, and move on.

The Ragman's Daughter
Donna Finney

On late Friday summer afternoons in my old Bronx neighborhood we would all hear the familiar cry of the Ragman: "*Vecchi vestiti, stracci! Vecchi vestiti, stracci!*" and take cover. It wasn't just the fact that he was dirty and grimy, but it was that screechy, *whiny* call that sounded like he was calling the dead spirits to join in behind him that made us run for our lives.

We were all afraid of him, including my cousins, Salvatore and Sally. I think their mom, my Aunt Vera, used it as a threat when they wouldn't mind her. I remember hearing her say, "You better watch out, Salvatore; I'm gonna tell the Ragman to come here and take you away!" I don't think he ever believed her, but it scared the daylights out of poor little Sally.

This one scorching hot day in July, Salvatore dared me and Sally to follow the Ragman, leading us past the familiar aroma of Cassello's Bakery and between the colorful rows of fresh fruits and vegetables and the smell of the fish carts on either side. We rounded the corner, on our old bikes, to a dingy alley that my papa told me never to go down. I followed reluctantly with Sally, tagging along behind.

"Are you crazy?" I shook my head. "Why would we want to follow *him*?"

"To see where he lives!"

"Well, I'm not goin' with ya."

"Suit yourself. You're not supposed to be near this alley to start with, so I hope your dad catches you!" He pedaled ahead. "You're comin' with me, Sally. I'm your older brother, and you're supposed to listen to me."

"I want to go home!" Sally whined as the tears streamed down her face.

"Stop being such a baby," he said.

It didn't take much for Sally to cry, but it always got to me, and I always gave in. "Alright, I'll go with you. Come on, Sally." I pulled my bike beside her and wiped the tears from her face with my shirt sleeve.

I guess I knew better, but I didn't want Sally to go by herself with him. I have to admit that curiosity got the best of me too, *and* I hated for Salvatore to beat me at a dare, so we all started pedaling our bikes down the street after him.

"He's going to get us if he turns around." She was barely able to speak the words, as her little feet pedaled, slowing down with every turn.

"Shut up, Sally! Pedal harder or he *will* get you!" Salvatore always talked to his sister that way. He was my older cousin, and I looked up to him most of the time, but sometimes I got tired of him badgering little Sally, who was only six years old. I was ten, and Salvatore was almost a year older. Sally never could keep up with us, though she tried.

Clickety-clack-ee-eeh, clickety-clack-ee-eeh. We could hear the squeak of the old wagon in the distance as the wheels turned and the tired horse pulled it down the dusty gray street. "*Vecchi vestiti, stracci!*"

Sally said, "Why does his voice sound like that? He sounds like a scary pirate!"

"Aarrr," yelled Salvatore. He held an imaginary sword up to poor Sally, but it all seemed real. Today we were running from an enemy of the people. Uncle Sal and Papa said that they heard he was from the old country and a *Sicilian*, where most of the criminals were from.

"I don't know, Sally, maybe he got in an accident," I said. I had to agree that I wondered about his raspy tone too.

"Maybe his throat's been cut out, or maybe he was forced to drink some kind of gasoline by some notorious Sicilian gangster, so he wouldn't spill the beans." Salvatore skidded his bike to a stop at the end of the alley.

"What does 'spill the beans' mean?" Sally's eyes were wide as an owl's.

"It means don't be a tattle tale, stupid," Salvatore said.

"Is that all he knows how to say? What does it mean?" whispered Sally.

"Sally, I can't believe you don't know what it means. Just look at him." Salvatore pointed.

"Leave her alone, Salvatore. He is yelling 'Old Clothes!' and then

'Rags!'"

"Why does he want our old clothes?"

"I guess because it's his job, and . . . well, I don't know. I'll ask my mama, later," I said.

"Shh . . . he's almost there!" Salvatore motioned for us to look ahead.

We could still see the wagon up ahead as Salvatore waved frantically for us to catch up. I would pedal and then wait for Sally . . . pedal and wait. As we got closer to the park, there was a beautiful stream, and people were wading in the water. We could see a small waterfall in the distance that was at the southeast end of the park.

Sally said, "Look at the people swimming! Can we go in the water?"

I remembered Papa's voice echoing in my ears. "The water's dangerous, Sally," I said. Salvatore gestured for us to follow him.

Sally could barely push the heavy pedals, and I said, "Salvatore, let's go back." I pointed to Sally. "We're both too tired and can't make this hill."

Salvatore said, "Look, he's going left. Let's put down our bikes."

We watched as the rag-wagon came to a stop at a tiny old shack. It was standing in a clearing in front of us. The boards were all jagged and gray, and some had holes the size of quarters. The windows were covered with an array of dull colored material. There was a door built with heavy lumber that resembled an oak tree. On the side of the house, there was a thin wire fence that kept two goats and a few chickens. Clothes hung on a line between two trees, including gray cloth diapers and rags. As we headed toward the shack, we saw the Ragman tie his horse to another tree. He turned around, as if he heard a noise, and we ducked behind the thick mulberry bushes.

Salvatore ran to the side of the shack and signaled for me and Sally to join him. I grabbed Sally's hand, and we made a run for it, slouching down next to Salvatore. The rag curtains on that end of the house were drawn neatly to one side, and we could see in as he entered the dwelling. Two little children called, "Papa, Papa," grabbing his legs.

A girl with long black hair said, "*Mia bello papa.*" She was facing us, and we could see that she had blue eyes as warm as the color of the sky on a sunny day and a bright smile to match. Salvatore stared, and Sally was as mesmerized as I was.

A short, plump woman ran up to him from the opposite direction. She had a kerchief around her dark hair and was holding a little boy with just a rag diaper on. We couldn't see her face, but we could see the Ragman reach out his arms to hug her. "Papa," she said as she tried to compete with the little bodies below her. She pointed to her huge stomach, and he pointed to his sack. He looked like Santa Claus from the side as he removed his sack from his back. He reached in and pulled out a loaf of bread.

The Ragman kissed his wife on the mouth and then kissed the baby on the forehead, "*Mama, mia bella.*" I didn't notice the raspy tone in his voice as he whispered the sweet words. I didn't notice his grimy face and tattered clothes. His voice got a little firmer as he said, "*Angelina, posso avere del'acqua?*"

"*Si, Papa,*" said the girl and headed toward the door.

Salvatore whispered, "Let's go!" and grabbed Sally's hand as they ran into the woods. I was frozen. My legs felt like tree stumps.

The girl, Angelina, was turning from the front of the house to the side of the house holding a metal pail. I was still crouched down; my legs were now like heavy anchors. I tried to move them, but they had their own mind and had decided between them that they were going nowhere.

"*Mama mia!*" she said as she rounded the corner and saw me squatted on the ground. I stood up and smiled.

"*Ciao,*" I said quietly and put my fingers to my lips, afraid that her parents would hear.

"*Cosa si fai qui?*" whispered the girl.

Why *am* I here? I did not want to explain the real reason why I was there, so I just said, "I'm lost . . . I mean . . . uh . . . *Mi sono perso.*" That might have been true, if Salvatore left me behind.

"*Vieni con me.*" She motioned for me to come, as she walked toward the stream and scooped out a pail of water. She gestured for me to follow her again back to the house. "*No . . . aspetta qui.*" I stayed on the side of the house and watched her go in.

The mama handed him some old rags. "*Grazie mia bella.*" He turned to Angelina and hugged her. "*Grazie mia bella figlia.*" When he opened his eyes after wiping his face, they were the same dazzling blue color as his older daughter's. I was astonished and ashamed at the same time . . . ashamed to think of all the mean, scary things we had all said about him. He was not a murderer or a criminal or any type of bad man at all. He was just a papa, like my papa, trying to feed his family.

Angelina walked out of the door and back to the side of the house, smiling as she turned the corner, "*Mia amica? Dove stai andando? Ti sei perso?*"

"No, I know where I'm going, and I'm not really lost. I have to catch up to my friends." I pointed to the woods. "Oh, sorry, I don't know that much Italian. *Non, parlo bene l'italiano.*" Realizing that I had used up most of my Italian words, I pointed to the woods again, "*I miei amici,*" and took her hand to follow me.

"No, ah . . . ." She pointed to the house. "*Mia papa.*" I nodded. I knew how she felt. My papa was just as concerned about me, like most Italian fathers who were obsessed about their girls' safety on the streets. I really wanted her to meet my friends, though. "*Per favore, i miei amici.*" I pulled her hand.

We both ran, hand-in-hand, giggling as I led her to where the bikes were. I only hoped that Salvatore had waited. When I got to the big oak tree, he and Sally were sitting on the ground, examining the egg-like nuts and peeling their shells to see what was inside. "It's about time. We almost left ya," he said. He looked up, startled to see Angelina with me. "What's *she* doing here?"

"I wanted to introduce you. Angelina, *permette che le presenti*, Salvatore, this is Angelina." He stood up and bowed like a grown gentleman.

Sally poked me in the leg. "What about *me*?"

"Oh, I can't forget about you. Angelina, this is little Sally," I said, forgetting my Italian.

"*Oh, scusate, permette che le presenti un poco mia amica, Sally.*"

Sally bowed as if she had a fancy dress on.

Angelina giggled, "*Piacere di conoscerti, mi chiamo Angelina Aliprandi.*" She bowed. Then she pointed to me. "*E come ti chiami?*"

"Oh, I forgot about me!" I laughed. She looked perplexed, and I added quickly, "*Mi chiamo Anne Marie Benenati.*" I bowed, and she curtsied back. Her dress that was made out of rags seemed quite elegant, and we all laughed, except for Salvatore. He just had that familiar scowl on his face.

"Well, it's been nice to meet ya, too, but we need to get back home before we get whipped by *our* papas. You know, *una fustigazione!* I know that word pretty well, because of Poppie."

"*Oh, si, si, anch'io.*" She pointed in the direction of the shack. "*Ciao,*" she said. She waved goodbye and started to walk back.

We all shouted in unison, "*Ciao!*"

Then she turned around "*Mia amica?*" Her eyes were sparkling with anticipation.

"*Oh, si, mia amica!*" I shouted.

"*Si, mia amica!*" she sang as she ran down the path in the opposite direction.

"Anne Marie, why does her mama have a big stomach?" Sally asked.

"She is going to have another baby." She looked like she was going to ask me another question, but I didn't want to answer *that* one.

"Did you see that Mr. Aliprandi has eyes as blue as hers?"

They both looked at me and said in unison, "Who?!"

"Mr. Aliprandi, you know, her father, the Ragman. She must get her looks from her papa."

"How could you think that she looks like the Ragman? He's gross!" Salvatore said. "She's *beautiful.*"

"Well, ya never know, 'cous,'" I said, winking.

"Aw, shut up." He grabbed his bike. "Let's go." We all got on our bikes and rode the long way home, back through the forest, the park, and the alley to Southern Blvd and then 183rd Street. All the way home I pedaled and would wait for Sally . . . pedal and wait. With each pause, I'd see Angelina and her family . . . especially the moment when *he* walked in the door, with that sack over his back. I smiled and shook my head. I couldn't believe that today I had seen where the Ragman lived and met his daughter, a new friend.

"Come on, Sally, *mama mia!* We're gonna be in trouble!"

"*Una fustigazione?*" said Sally's breathless voice.

"That's right, a big spanking!"

"Hurry up, you two, or I'm gonna tell on you," said Salvatore.

"Are you gonna spill the beans?" Sally said.

Salvatore stopped his bike to wait up for us. "Naw, I'm not a tattle tale, stupid." He winked and looked both ways as he crossed the street.

We were nearing Cassello's Bakery, and I could smell the bread as my stomach growled. We hurried past the stands of glowing red and green apples. Past the carts that were closing for the day, loaded with cucumbers, onions, and peppers. Past the lingering stink of trout and bass hanging from the fish cart. I wished I had some way of bringing that food back to her family, but then that meant that I would have to tell Mama and Papa the whole story.

We stopped in front of the eight steps that led to our little apartment, and Salvatore and Sally said, *"Ciao"* as they walked over to the next door.

"Ciao." I went up the steps, slowly leading my bike to the hallway.

My papa yelled, "Anne Marie, where were you? It's almost time for dinner. Come and help your mother with the pasta."

"Si, mi bello papa." I ran to him and gave him a big hug.

I sang dreamily, *"Mia amica. Mia nuovo amica."*

"Mia amica? Your new friend? Who is that?"

Now was my chance to tell him. Should I let him know where I'd been? Then I answered decidedly, "The Ragman's daughter, Papa."

He looked at me with an inquisitive eyebrow. Then he just smiled and said, *"Mia bella figlia,* now you are telling tales."

"No, Papa, it really is the truth. She is very nice and beautiful and has blue eyes the color of the summer sky after it rains and long dark hair that reaches her waist . . ."

Mama came over to the table, holding little Joey in her arms. "Oh, my lilla Anna Maria, sucha *narrator,* sucha, how you say, Papa . . . imagination."

Papa smiled and said, "Yes, some day she will be a great storyteller."

"Really, Papa, I want to help them."

"Help who? Oh, Anne Marie, *vieni mangiare, mia figlia dolce."* He winked at Mama.

"Anna Maria, *mangia,*" said Mama, as she put little Joey in his feeding chair and gave him his bowl of cut up pasta.

My stomach growled again, reminding me that Mama was right. I sat down and picked up the bread from Cassello's. Maybe tomorrow I could bring Papa and Mama past the bakery, the stands, and the smelly fish cart. Maybe I could lead them down the dingy alley that I wasn't supposed to go down. I took a bite of the soft bread and stared at my pasta. How could I make Mama and Papa believe me? How could I get them to help me?

80

"Anne Marie, *mangia*," Mama said. I picked up my fork and twisted the pasta around the ends and put it to my mouth. Maybe tomorrow.

The next morning I got up early and wandered out to the kitchen to help Mama. Joey was in his high chair, stirring his little finger in his oatmeal.

"Anna Maria, you uppa early."

"Yes, Mama. I want to talk to you about my friend Angelina and her family."

"Who?" She cut the bread for toast.

"Angelina, the Ragman's daughter."

"Oh, Anna Maria, you are sucha *narrator*. You justa want *una amico*. You know you mada one uppa when you were about five. Now, just becuzza we mova, you thinka you need one. School will start soon and you will meeta some new friends. Stoppa with the stories."

"Mama, I'm not making up an imaginary friend. She is for real. You can ask Salvatore and Sally." I put the cup on the table for Mama's coffee.

"Oh, pleasa, Anna Maria, you wanta me to believa your cousins? They make uppa stories all the time." She poured the coffee into her cup.

"Mama, listen. Yesterday, Salvatore dared me and Sally to follow the Ragman to see where he lives so . . ."

"Whata? You listen to Salvatore?"

"Yes, that's what I've been trying to tell you. We went down 183rd, you know where that alley is?" I buttered the toast, taking care to put extra butter on mine.

"You meana the one you not supposed to go downa? Your papa is gonna be mada. He gonna give you *una fustigazione*!"

"Mama, I don't care!" I slapped down the butter knife.

"Anna Maria!"

"But Mam, the Ragman is a real man with a real name. His name is Mr. Aliprandi, and he has three little children and Angelina."

"*Chi e Angelina?*" She took a sip from her coffee.

"She is the Ragman's daughter. See! You're not listening. We followed him out past the big park, and they all live in this old shack. The windows have rags for curtains, and the baby wears diapers that are made out of old rags. He brought them a loaf of bread, and they looked *so*

81

hungry! We've got to help them! You have to help me tell Papa!"

"Anna Maria. Your papa is gonna be mada. You went downa the alley and to the biga parka." She cut up little bits of toast and put them on Joey's high chair, then turned to face me.

"Mama, please, listen to me. I want to teach her English and help them. They are Italian just like us!"

"Noa, they are notta just lika us. We comma to this country to worka hard and be Americans, but they comma to this country to taka from people. Your papa said he heard they are Sicilians. Very bada people." Her face was red, and she tapped my arm. "You stay away froma them." She spoon fed Joey's dirty grinning face. "Now *mangia!*"

"But Mama . . ." She pointed her finger for me to sit down and eat. I knew that *that* was the end of the conversation.

The door opened slowly in mid-afternoon, and I thought Papa was home early, but it was Aunt Vera. She always walked into our house like she lived there, especially when she knew my papa was at work.

"Teresa? Anna Maria, where is your mama?" She glanced down the hall.

"She is putting Joey in for a nap."

She had that sheepish *I'm your Aunt Vera, and I'm gonna get you in trouble this time*, grin on her face. "Well, Anna Maria. Sally said she had to spill the beans."

"What do you mean?" I got up from the couch. *Looks like she's tryin' to get me in trouble again.*

"You know what I mean. Salvatore said you dared him to follow the Ragman to his house, and all of you went past the big park."

I just shook my head. *Salvatore is such a liar, and he will blame anybody so he won't have to get a beating.*

"Well, wait 'til I tell your mama. Poor Sally had bad dreams last night."

Mama entered the room. "*Vera, ciao. Cosa c'e'?*" she said, pouring herself another cup of coffee. "*Una taza di café?*"

"No, no coffee for me today, although God knows I couldn't sleep last night. Sally had bad dreams, and it's all because Anna Maria dared Salvatore and Sally to ride their bikes and follow the Ragman yesterday." She turned to me with that maddening grin again.

"Noa, my Anna Maria would notta do that. She saida Salvatore dared her." Mama shook her head firmly, but her eyes looked questionably at me.

"He knows he would get a beating if he did that. He is afraid of his Poppie." Aunt Vera slapped her hands together, which made Mama and me jump.

Just then my Papa walked through the door. He greeted Mama with a kiss and looked at Aunt Vera, "You causin' trouble again, Vera?" He always talked to his sister in that half kidding tone.

"No, but your daughter is. My Salvatore said your Anna Maria made him and Sally follow the Ragman, down the alley and past the big park."

Papa turned from Aunt Vera to me. "What? Anna Maria is this true?"

"Well, no, well, actually yes . . . we went there . . . that's what I was trying to tell you—"

"What? You went down the alley? Past the park?" His face was as red as Mama's was earlier.

"Papa, I was trying to tell you last night. We followed the Ragman, and they live in a shack and are really poor. They have no food and—," I swallowed hard.

"You disobeyed my orders?"

"Papa, I uh, well, Salvatore dared us . . ."

"I don't want to hear that you would listen to a dare." He started to take off his belt.

Mama went over to him, "Noa, Vincenzo, she was trying to tella me this morning that Salvatore dared her. She metta these pora people."

"Well, I better be going." Aunt Vera shuffled toward the door.

"Yeah, go ahead and start trouble and then leave, Vera. Well, I hope that you're going to punish Salvatore for daring my daughter. You know that *she* would never have dared *him*, Vera. They should *all* be in trouble." Aunt Vera walked out backwards, raising her hands up.

"Come here, Anne Marie." Papa had his belt wound around his hand.

"I'm sorry, Papa. I was wrong, I know. I tried to tell you, but you didn't believe me."

Papa put down his belt. "Do you know how dangerous that alley is? Do you know that people have gotten beat up in that park worse than any

83

beating I could ever give you? What do you think I should do?"

"Listen to me, Papa. You're always telling me that we need to help other people. The Ragman and his family are very poor. Would you let me show you where they live?"

Papa put down his belt. "Anne Marie, I believe you now, but I'm very disappointed in you. I'm not going to spank you, but I want you to promise me that you will never go out there again."

"Papa, why can't we help them?"

"Because I said so. Do not go out there again. They are bad people. They are *Sicilians*!" He turned around and walked toward the bathroom. I knew I was defeated. I really wished that he had given me a spanking that day because it would have felt better than the sadness that was in my heart.

Over a week went by. I was grounded and not allowed to ride my bike or play with Salvatore or Sally. I sat in my room and read a book that my teacher gave me right before school was out called *The Wizard of Oz*. I had seen the movie on our new black and white TV last year, and no one had believed poor Dorothy, either. I wondered if Mama and Papa believed me. If they did, then they wouldn't want little children to go hungry. Dorothy ended up running away. I didn't think I could do that. I put on the radio and heard two beautiful voices singing, as the announcer said, "'I'll Do My Cryin' in the Rain' by the Everly Brothers." That's what I was doing for a week, and it hasn't helped anyone. Maybe I needed to be more like Dorothy. I needed to be brave. I left my radio on as I quietly shut my bedroom door.

I saw Mama rocking little Joey, half asleep in the rocking chair by their bed. She would never know it if I snuck out. I stuffed my little shoulder bag with some fresh fruit and cookies Mama had made the night before. I shut the door quietly, grabbed my bike, and heading down the stairs.

I made my way to the alley and held my breath as I sped through it. The rain was falling lightly, and I almost slipped when I rounded the corner. I pedaled my way up to where the park was and stopped. Did I really want to do this? If I brought this food to Angelina, I could drop it off and head back before Papa came home and Mama noticed me missing. I continued pedaling. I had tied my hair with a bandana, and rain was dripping down my face, but I didn't care. I got to the front of the shack and knocked on the door.

Angelina came to the door. "*Mia amica! Ci fai qui?*" She led me inside, and her three little siblings chatted excitedly around me in Italian. The mama went and got some rags for me to dry myself off with.

I thanked her and reached in my bag. "*Per voi.*"

"Oh, *Noa* . . ." said the mama.

"Mama!" Angelina turned to me. "*Grazie,*" and handed the cookies to her three siblings.

"*Grazie!*" said the mama. Just then, the papa came through the door.

"*Cosa fa lei qui?*" He was wet and weary, and his voice had that screechy sound.

I trembled. Angelina said, "Papa!" She started rambling in Italian some words that I couldn't understand. His voice grumbled as he took the bag of food and handed it back to me.

I didn't know what to do or say. The mama nodded apologetically. "*Mi dispiaci.*"

Angelina thanked me, and we walked outside. It had stopped raining, and the sun was starting to find its way back in the afternoon sky. I looked at Angelina. "*Mi dispiaci.*"

"*Noa, Mi dispiaci mia amica.* My papa . . . uh . . . *no capire.*"

"I know, and I'm sorry, too. I didn't mean to insult you or your family. I was only trying to help." She had a puzzled look on her face. I just shrugged. "*Ciao, mia amica.*"

"*Ciao!*" she said.

I took off on my bike through the woods, but I didn't get too far. I slipped in the mud near that oak tree where Salvatore and Sally had waited for me. "Ow!" I yelled. I had landed on my right ankle, and I felt a stabbing pain. My clothes were all muddy, and I was soaked. I didn't know what to do. I sat for a minute. Maybe if I yelled for help they could hear me. I wasn't that far away. "Help! Someone help me!" What was the word in Italian? "*Aiuti! Aiuti!*"

In a few minutes, I saw Angelina running through the woods. "*Mia amica! Aspetti!*" and motioned for me to wait. Where was I gonna go? All I could think of was *Boy, am I in trouble now! I'm sure that I will get it, not only a spanking, but be grounded for the rest of the summer.*

Angelina came back with her papa. He looked at me sternly, and I shuddered, but this time mostly from the pain and drops of wet, messy mud that was slithering down into my eyes. He wiped off my eyes with his shirt and picked me up gently, taking me back in their shack. Angelina got a basin of water, and the mama helped to wash the dirt off me. My ankle was already swelling up, and the mama went outside and got some mud to put on it.

My papa was probably almost home by now, and I wonder if Mama noticed me missing. *What was I thinking?*

I said to Angelina, "*Mia Mama and Papa*" and pointed outside.

"*Si,*" She pointed to her papa. She said something to her papa, and he nodded. He carried me outside and loaded my bike and me on the cart with him. I motioned for Angelina to come, and she asked her papa. He nodded, and she sat in the wagon next to me, and we waved goodbye to the mama and children.

It seemed like such a long ride back. I directed him to my street and pointed to my house, and he pulled his wagon in front. He took me out of the wagon, and Angelina got my bike. We headed up the steps, and he knocked.

My mama and papa answered the door, "Anna Maria!" Mama said.

They were both shocked to see the Ragman standing there holding me.

"Mama! Papa! I'm so sorry. I went to bring them food, and I fell and . . ."

The Ragman handed me over to my papa, who took me and put me on the couch.

"Papa, this is Mr. Aliprandi and Angelina." Papa had that stern look still in his eyes, but Mama ran over and said, "*Piaciare*" and reached out her hand to both of them. "*Grazi,*" she said. "*Calmati,*" she said to Papa, patting him on the arm.

He looked at them both and finally broke out that old smile. "*Grazi . . . Piaciare!*" Angelina looked at me and smiled. I grinned. Even though I was in pain, it was all worth it now.

The next day Papa took me to the doctor. I had a sprained ankle and was grounded for two weeks for my disobedience, but both Papa and Mama began to soften after meeting Mr. Aliprandi. Papa and Mama rode me out there after church the following Sunday, and after that, we made it part of our Sunday ritual to eat lunch with them. Mama loved to bring her cake and Italian crème cookies, and Papa would bring a chicken and some fruit to trade with Mr. Aliprandi for the vegetables in his garden. I would read to Angelina and her brothers: Alfonso; the older one, named after his papa; and Alberto, the younger one, named after his uncle.

By the end of the summer, Angelina seemed to be catching on to English, along with her brothers. I had asked my papa if we could talk to the school about how to get them into classes, and he said that he would talk to Aunt Vera. She knew everyone, including the lady in the office.

We were all excited when Angelina's mother, Maria Angelina, had the baby in August and it was a girl. Angelina said that they named it Anna Maria, after me, because her mama said I was *una benedizione*, which is the Italian word for a blessing.

One Sunday after church, we drove out there and found the shack deserted. I wondered what could have happened. Mama and Papa said that maybe they had been discovered out there and were forced to move. There were only a few old rags hanging on the windows. It reminded me of *The Diary of Anne Frank*, another book I was reading at the end of the summer. She was a young girl about my age who was also very close to her Papa. We shared the same name, but this time Angelina was the brave one who had to move on.

It made me wonder about our names, so one Saturday before school started, I had Papa take me to the big library. We had the lady at the desk help us look up my first name, which *did* mean blessing, but I found out that my last name, Benenati, meant born good. My papa just nodded, "Yes, we are from a good family, Anne Marie."

Then I had the lady look up Angelina's last name, "Aliprandi means born by a Saint." She looked up from the book. "Who is born by a Saint?" My papa and I said at the same time, "The Ragman's daughter!"

I begged Papa to find out where they were, but we never found out what happened to them. *Mia amica*, Angelina was gone from my life as mysteriously as she appeared, along with the rest of her family.

* * *

One late Friday morning, near the end of that school year, I thought I heard a screechy sound, but it was just a stray cat outside my window. How I longed for the days when I heard that familiar cry. I turned on the radio and listened to the Everly Brothers harmonizing "Bye, Bye Love" as a ray of sunshine streamed across the room. I thought of her sparkling eyes and smile—the Ragman's daughter.

"*Mia amica*," I said softly. Just then, a cloud passed over, and the sunlight faded as quickly as it came.

Josie's Special Delivery
Michelle Lansdale

The first thing I thought when I woke up was it was Saturday, and Saturday meant I didn't have to go to school, and I usually got to see Walter. The first thing I heard was my mom's muffled voice coming from another room in the house. Then I heard a man's voice. I figured it must be Bennie—one of my mom's boyfriends. He was the only one she ever let stay overnight. Mom said she left my real dad when I was a baby, so I had no idea who he was or what he might look like.

I lay there for a few minutes, staring at the peeling, pink paint on the window-sill. I reached over and flicked some of the loose paint off, revealing a pale shade of green on top of a royal blue. I wondered if any other thirteen-year-old girls ever lived in this room and what they were like. Walter said I was lucky to have my own room.

Harley, my dog, trotted over to me and started licking my face. We took Harley in after one of mom's boyfriends left him at our house. I think he's part husky; he looks like a wolf. He sticks to me like glue. I think Harley likes me better than he likes anyone else.

I could tell from the way Mom and Bennie talked that they were not arguing, so I decided it was safe to get out of bed. I shuffled into the kitchen and saw my mom and Bennie sitting at the kitchen table. There was a scale, a box of Ziploc baggies, and a big bag of weed sitting in front of Mom and Bennie. Mom had been selling weed for a long time, but she stopped hiding it from me when I started middle school last year. One time, she told me that she figured I was old enough to know the truth, and then she told me I shouldn't tell anyone or else I may end up living in a foster home. Walter told me he would see to it that I'd never have to live in a foster home. But I wasn't so much worried about living in a foster home as I was about my friends finding out my mom was a drug dealer—that would be too embarrassing. After spending a lot of weekends at home while all my friends went to the movies and stuff, I finally realized they already knew about my mom's drug dealing. Of course, I found that out the hard way after my best friend's mom wouldn't let her spend the night. My best friend's mom was afraid the cops would raid our house in the middle of the night. After that, my friends and I just met at the mall on the weekends. I was okay with that because I figured it was better than nothing.

As I made my way toward the pantry, my mom said, "Morning, Josie!" Mom was always full of energy, even first thing in the morning.

As I opened the back door to let Harley out, I replied, "Hey, Mom. Is that my shirt?"

She was wearing a pink, rhinestone t-shirt, about two sizes too small, which had the words *Girls Just Wanna Have Fun* on the front, a denim mini-skirt, and hot-pink stilettos. The front of the t-shirt was tied in a knot so it showed off her cheap belly-button ring. Her platinum blonde hair was teased toward heaven, and her chocolate roots were starting to show. My mom was skinny and in her early thirties, but she dressed like she was eighteen. She embarrassed me when she dressed like that, but I didn't say anything because I didn't want to cause one of her crying spells.

"Oh, I don't know, maybe. Is it? You don't mind, do you?" She poked her chest out and looked down.

"Nah, I don't care," I lied, "I think I spilled pink Kool-Aid on it last week anyway."

Bennie never looked up from the table. He never really spoke to me much unless he wanted me to make him a sandwich or something. My mom always said that Bennie looked like he stepped out of "Starsky and Hutch." I'd never seen that show, but I guessed I needed to so I'd know what she was talking about. Bennie's stringy, sandy hair was a little past his shoulders, and he had what my mom called a "porn moustache." He was wearing bell-bottom jeans, a white t-shirt, a tan leather jacket, and a big gold chain around his neck—the same thing he wore just about every day.

"Hey, Bennie," I said, just to make him speak to me.

"Hey," he grunted without looking at me.

"Josie, honey," Mom said. "I'm gonna need you to make a run over to Walter's house around noon. It's eleven o'clock now."

Bennie looked up at me. Our eyes met for about two seconds; then he looked back at the table and just stared at it for several seconds before he went back to bagging weed.

I put two cherry pop-tarts into the toaster and said, "Sure, no problem."

Walter was the old man who fronted the weed for Mom. He gave the weed to her, she sold it, I brought the money to Walter, and he gave me more weed to bring back to Mom. I did this every Saturday, like clockwork. Mom said it was easier for me to bring the money to Walter because no one would think I was a drug dealer.

Walter was okay, I guess. He was tall—taller than Bennie. He limped when he walked, and Mom said that she heard he lost part of one of his legs in a motorcycle accident. She said it served him right. I had no idea why she didn't like him. He was bald, but not because he was old. I think he shaved all his hair off. Going to his house was not a bad thing because Walter was always nice to me. Plus, I got to get out of the house for a little while. I always knocked on Walter's back door instead of the front—we had a secret-code-knock. Sometimes, Marcus was at Walter's house when I'd go over there, and he'd answer the door. Marcus was a friend of Walter's, and he was a scary looking guy. Marcus was younger than Walter and much taller. His arms were covered in tattoos and bigger than my legs. He even had a couple of teardrop tattoos under his left eye.

Right inside the back door was Walter's kitchen, and it was always clean: not like our kitchen. The cabinets were painted yellow, and usually a bowl of fruit sat on the kitchen table —sometimes it was full of red apples, sometimes bananas, and sometimes both. Walter usually asked me if I was hungry, then he'd nod toward the fruit.

"Go on and getcha some," he'd say.

Walter even let Harley in the house because Walter had a big dog too (a Rottweiler, I think), and they sniffed each other while I waited. A small TV sat on the kitchen counter, and lots of times Walter flipped the channel to cartoons. I watched the cartoons while Walter took the money into the next room. Then, he'd come back with a brown bag, and I'd put it in my backpack. I never looked in the bag, but I knew what was in it. Sometimes, he'd even give me a ten dollar bill and tell me that I shouldn't spend it all in one place. I usually stopped at the diner on the way home, and I'd buy a burger and an ice cream. See, that's why I said that Walter is okay by me.

After the pop-tarts were toasted, I let Harley back in and made my way to the living room sofa. I turned on the TV and shared one of my pop-tarts with Harley. From the sofa, I could still see and hear Mom and Bennie.

Bennie pulled Mom into his lap and said, "Gonna take me out tonight, Sugah Mamma?"

She giggled and said, "Sure, we had a good week. How about we celebrate at the ice house?"

"I'll go anywhere's you go, as long as you're buyin'," he laughed as he played with her belly-button ring. She giggled and squirmed in his lap. I turned up the volume on the TV. Harley growled, and he looked at Mom and Bennie.

"It's okay, boy. He's not hurting her. They're just playing," I whispered.

Harley laid his head down between his paws and closed his eyes.

I purposely interrupted. "Hey, Mom. A bunch of my friends are going to the mall tonight. Can I go?"

Quickly, I could tell that she was frustrated. She pushed Bennie's hand off of her stomach, sighed deeply, and said, "Not tonight, Josie. We're going out, and I don't want to have to pick you up."

"Oh, it's okay! I'm sure I can get a ride from someone," I said.

She closed her eyes and shook her head like she did when she had her mind made up, and said, "Not tonight, honey. You need to stay here and watch the house while we're out. I'll take you to the mall sometime this week, okay? Just you and me on a girl's day out. How's that sound?"

"Like it makes me want to throw-up," I whispered.

Mom raised her voice and walked toward me and Harley, "What's that, honey? I can't hear you over the TV."

"I said, I can't wait to grow up," I raised my voice, but I never took my eyes off the TV. To keep myself out of trouble, I shoved half a pop-tart in my mouth.

"Don't rush it, honey. You'll always be my little Rosie Josie," she said while pinching my cheek.

* * *

When I got out of the shower, Mom was sitting at the kitchen table, painting her nails.

"Where's Bennie?" I asked.

She blew her gum into a big pink bubble until it popped. After peeling the gum off of her lips with her tongue, she replied, "Oh, he said he was gonna run down to the diner and get us some lunch. He'll be right back."

"Okay," I said, "I'm headed to Walter's."

"Come on back when you're finished. I want you back before Bennie and me go out tonight," she said as she blew me a kiss.

I put on my red hoodie and called for Harley. I didn't bother putting a leash on him. He wouldn't leave my side for anything. Besides, I don't think we even owned a leash.

Walter's house was about a mile and a half away if I stayed on the main sidewalk, but I always cut through the old neighborhood park. It seemed faster, or maybe it was just that I liked to make something fun out of my trip. The best part about that park was that no one else was ever there—not since the new park across town was built. No one took care of the old park. The grass grew tall in the summer, and some of the swings were broken, but I liked having the park all to myself.

About a year ago, there was a big metal gate that someone put up to keep people out, but some older kids from the neighborhood cut the lock off the gate, so now anyone could just walk into the park at any time. On the other side of the park, there was another gate. It had the locks cut off of it too, and that was the exit we took to get to Walter's house.

After walking about three blocks, Harley and I rounded the corner into the park. We walked right through the entrance, and the first thing we heard was a squeaking noise. The first thing we saw was someone slowly spinning on the merry-go-round. The merry-go-round was small, probably made for little kids, so I could tell right away that the person was a grown-up. Harley and I stopped, and Harley growled. Then I realized that it was Bennie on the merry-go-round, so I patted Harley on the head and walked over to the merry-go-round.

Bennie looked toward us and smirked. He didn't seem surprised to see us. I figured that he knew my route to Walter's house and that he must have needed to tell me something.

"Hey, Bennie," I said.

"Sup?" he replied, still slowly spinning.

"On my way to Walter's. What are you doing here? Mom said you were picking up some lunch."

"Yeah, well, I suppose your mom can fend for herself," Bennie said.

I wrinkled my forehead in confusion, and replied, "What do you mean? Are you guys fighting...again?"

He chuckled, "Nah, we ain't fighting. I just don't think she'll like me much after today. Hell, she really doesn't like me all that much anyway."

Thoughts rushed into my mind as I tried to make sense of what Bennie was saying—or not saying. But my gut told me that Bennie was acting creepier than usual.

Harley stood at my side, and I kicked some pebbles around with my sneaker.

"Well, I gotta get over to Walter's house. He knows I'm on my way," I said.

Still spinning, Bennie traced a circle in the dirt with his shoe until the merry-go-round came to a stop. Harley and I stood about four feet away from Bennie as he looked me in the eyes. He seemed fidgety and chewed on his lip a lot.

"Now, you know I've never been mean to you," he said.

"Sure, sure, I know, and I know that you really don't like me either," I replied.

"So, this is not personal, but I'm gonna have to ask you to hand over that wad of money you got in your backpack."

I quickly looked toward the exit gate and back at Bennie. I put one hand on Harley's back and softly wrapped my hand around a fistful of his hair.

Looking at Bennie, Harley let out a deep, slow growl.

Bennie quickly stood up, took one step toward me, and looked down at Harley. Harley took one step back and barked.

Bennie stammered, "Okay now. Josie, I asked you nicely, but now I'm telling you to hand over that money. I'm not playing games, girl; give me the money." His hands shook as he pointed his finger at me.

At that time, we both heard two high-pitched shrieks coming from behind me. They startled both of us, and Bennie looked over my shoulder. Laughing and playing, two little girls passed the entrance to the park. Bennie closed his eyes and sighed.

I knew I had to do something. I took two steps forward, and as hard as I could, I kicked Bennie right between the legs.

Harley began barking like crazy. Bennie fell to his knees and doubled over into a fetal position. I could not believe that I really kicked him that hard, but I did!

Barking really loudly, Harley stood over Bennie and was salivating on Bennie's face. I darted for the exit.

I ran as fast as I could, and once I was about half a block away, I called for Harley. I heard Bennie shout two or three times.

Still running toward Walter's house, I kept looking behind me. I called for Harley again, and finally he came running out of the park, so I slowed down until he caught up with me.

Harley and I finally made it to Walter's back door, and I beat on the door again and again. I forgot our secret-code-knock.

Marcus came to the door, and after I caught my breath, I told him what happened.

"Wait here." Marcus looked pissed off, and he shut the door.

As I waited, I kneeled down beside Harley and hugged his neck. He licked my face, and I hugged him tighter. I'm glad that Mom's old boyfriend left Harley at our house.

Walter came out, and Marcus stood behind him.

"You okay?" Walter asked.

"Sure, sure. I'm okay. He really scared me...he's creepy, ya know? But I'm okay now," I replied.

Walter looked at Marcus and said, "That son-of-a-bitch has gone too far. You know what to do." Marcus headed for his truck.

Walter looked at me and said, "Come on, lil' lady. I'll walk you to the diner. You can buy me an ice-cream, and maybe the cook will have a steak bone for this wolf of yours." He handed me a twenty-dollar bill.

Before we headed for the diner, Walter said, "Hang on one minute. Wait right here." I could tell he was a little nervous, or angry, or something like that.

He limped over to Marcus's truck and looked back over his shoulder at me. I had no idea what he was saying, but Marcus revved the engine, and the tires squealed as he backed the truck out of the driveway. I didn't feel sorry for Bennie—not one bit.

* * *

When we got to the diner, I told Harley to wait outside. When we walked in, everyone said "hey" to Walter—the waitress, the cook, and an old man sitting on a barstool at the counter. Walter said "hey" back, and pointed to a booth near the front door. So, that's where we sat.

When the waitress came over, she pulled a pad of paper out of her bra and a pen out of her hair, and she said, "Burger and fries, Josie?"

"Nope. I think I want to change things up today," I answered. "I'll have the BLT and onion rings. Oh, and instead of coke, I want root beer, please." I could feel Walter watching me.

As she wrote down my order, she said, "What about you, Walter?"

Walter answered, "Uh...I'll have the same; that sounds good."

The waitress wrote it all down while looking from me to Walter. As she started walking off, Walter added, "Tell Lenny to toss the mutt a bone, would ya?"

"You got it, Daddy-O," she said with a wink.

Walter stared out the window, and I stared at Walter.

Something told me that it would be okay to talk to Walter about Bennie. I'd never told anyone about how I felt about him and about how I locked my door at night just to make sure that he didn't sneak into my room. I surely would never tell Mom. She always took Bennie's side in everything.

"So, Bennie really gives me the creeps. I don't like him, and I hate that he hangs around our house so much, ya know?"

"Really? Why is that? Has he done anything to you?" Walter asked. He was wringing his hands.

"Uh . . . no. He has not done anything, really. I just don't think he likes me. I try to stay in my room most of the time when he's there. And there was that one time when I woke up in the middle of the night, and I just felt like someone was watching me, ya know? But I was half asleep, so stuff didn't make much sense. I thought I saw a shadow standing by the door, but I just pulled the covers over my head. It wasn't until the next day when I saw Bennie sitting at the kitchen table that I realized that I had seen a light flash next to the door—I think it was Bennie's gold chain reflecting off of the light through the window."

Walter put his elbows on the table and held his head between his hands. He seemed to be thinking hard about what I just said. I was afraid that I said something wrong. Walter was really the only person who seemed to care about me, so I didn't want to make him mad or anything.

Then, he looked me straight in the eyes, and I swear I saw his eyes get all watery for a second.

"Listen, kid. There's something I have to tell you. Hold tight, okay? This may surprise you, but we'll get through this together, okay?" He pulled a pack of cigarettes out of his t-shirt pocket and lit one up.

My heart began to race, but I was curious at the same time. Then he took a couple drags off the cigarette and looked me in the eyes again.

"Your mom and me used to know each other a long time ago, before you were born," he said while shifting around in the booth. "In fact, we dated once, and...well...we were married once. I was there when you were born...if you know what I mean."

It took me a minute to figure out what he was telling me. I could feel him watching me, like he was waiting to see how I would react.

"I think I know what you're trying to tell me. So, you don't got to say it out loud," I said.

That's when the waitress brought our food. I was kinda glad that she came when she did. It gave me time to think before I said anything else.

Walter squirted ketchup all over his onion rings. I usually put the ketchup in a puddle on the side of my plate, but this time I squirted ketchup all over my onion rings, like Walter.

He looked a little sad, or disappointed, or something, so I figured I better go ahead and say what I was thinking. "So, I'm glad. I mean, I think it's cool. You have always been nice to me—a lot nicer than most people."

"I think, from now on, the whole world should be nice to you," he said. "You don't have to worry about Bennie any longer. He won't be bothering you again."

I smiled. I thought Walter was about to cry or something, but after a few seconds, he smiled and called the waitress over.

He told her, "Bring me a banana split, will ya?"

The waitress said, "What about you, Josie? Want that usual strawberry sundae?"

"Nope," I replied and put the twenty-dollar bill on the table, "Today I'll have a banana split."

I had no idea banana splits tasted so good.

A Place in the Choir

Ann Manes

All God's creatures got a place in the choir
Some sing low, some sing higher
Some sing out loud on the telephone wire
And some just clap their hands or paws or anything they got

Listen to the bass, that's the one on the bottom
Where the bullfrog croaks and the hippopotamus
Moans and groans with a big to-do
And the old cow just goes moo
                    —Bill Staines

    The Methodists of Bent Vine Creek worshipped in the Little Brown Church in the Vale. Though there was no actual vale, there was a little brown building surrounded by loblolly pines by Nature's design and azaleas by the pastor's wife's. Because the pastor placed great emphasis on singing (he himself led the bass section) and less on the collection as a sign of stewardship, there was a fair congregation at the Little Brown Church, and the choir consequently was decent. Their red choir robes had been donated by the First Methodist in Jasper when it upgraded and, if the choir sang without professionalism, it looked good and sang with great zeal.

    Pastor Fortenberry appreciated zeal. He preached with zeal; he visited the sick with zeal; he hunted with zeal. He had been zealous all his life, zealous in love, in hobbies, and in investments. Now, in relative retirement and due largely to the zealous investments, he was free to pursue his hunting. He had few pastoral duties; he had cut a sweet deal with the vestry of the Little Brown Church in the Vale. He preached, and he visited the sick; in return, he and Stella lived at the parsonage and drew a small stipend, enough for her to have money for her quilting. The vestry took care of the daily needs of the place.

    In his blind on his deer lease, Pastor Fortenberry thought about the beauty of nature whenever he drew a bead on the animals nibbling at the corn below the deer feeder. He had learned he was 1/128 Cherokee and believed he felt that blood pulse as he hunted, calling silently on the spirit of Deer as if his own survival depended on the trophy he had lured with bags of cracked corn, as if he would process the meat and mount the head himself, as if Stella did not have Market Basket's brisket and potato salad in the refrigerator.

There were always too many deer. They were a nuisance that either starved or ate people's gardens, and they depended entirely on humans for the culling of the herd, ridding them of those that kept the herd from being constant and healthy. Hunting was the Lord's work, and happily, Pastor Fortenberry enjoyed it.

"Lord, Thou givest them their meat in due season. Thank You, and thank You for the presence of this deer in my sights."

The stag buckled as the pastor had pictured it: he did not fall to the ground but stumbled and began to try to trot away from the sound that echoed around him, the sound that had come with the deep and searing ache in his shoulder. His instinct was to run to shelter to escape the pain that grew with every motion and minute that passed.

The buck moved as if confused. His head and neck were flecked with blood; his eyes darted. He stumbled toward the bushes where he had sheltered the night before. He jumped awkwardly as if he were trying to escape the smell of the blood, as if fear were having the same effect on him the hole in his lung was having, but the jump only drove the bullet deeper.

He entered the bushes, the ground there still slightly warm from his sleep. His front legs buckled, and despite the pain, he obeyed the instinct that told him to lie still and make no sound. He seemed to need the warmth and the smell he had made before the blood smell had begun.

And then he heard the footsteps that had tracked him.

> The dogs and the cats they take up the middle
> Where the honeybees hum and the crickets fiddle
> The donkey brays and the pony neighs
> And the old gray badger sighs

"It's okay, kitty," Tammy said. "It'll be fine. It'll all be better soon."

The feral tom spit and hissed from the live-trap. A deep yowl started in his throat as Tammy neared. Cat snot sprayed from his nose and mouth when she reached toward him, and the cat jerked from side to side, fighting the wires of the cage.

The cage handle was above the cat, and, when he saw Tammy's flesh, he went for it. Two scimitar claws dug into her hand between her thumb and forefinger, so deeply he could not retract them. Although Tammy was accustomed to claws and teeth—a gridwork of scar tissue ran from the middle of her flabby upper arms to the tips of her sometimes arthritic fingers—this tug was disabling. She let the trap go and jerked her hand away, and the claws tore through like a box cutter through packaging tape. Though it fell only a couple of feet, the jar of the drop popped the trap open. The cat struggled to get back through, but the mechanism sprang back again and caught the cat across the throat. Powered by a burst of adrenaline and on a downward slope, the squirming cat propelled the trap toward the creek, skittering it over pine needles and momentarily hanging on the root system of a downed pine tree. A final lunge by the panicked cat tipped the trap over the sandy ledge, and it submerged in the frigid, churning waters of Bent Vine Creek.

"Oh, my God," Tammy kept muttering as she slid down the embankment and stumbled after the trap. "Oh, kitty, oh, God."

Below the ledge the creek ran deep and swift from the recent winter rain. She saw the trap tumble, submerge, and bounce as she made her way to the sandbar some thirty yards away. The water still sped, but the trap slowed on the sandy bottom of the shallows. She stepped through the nearly knee-deep water, swinging her arms, her rubber boots not tall enough to keep the water out, and lunged after the trap. Ignoring the pain of the cold water and the searing pain in her torn hand, she dragged the trap to higher ground, knelt, and pulled on its door. The cat's head was caught by the door of the trap, and Tammy had to manipulate his body to free it. The cat was cold through, but he was beyond feeling winter's pinch. Tammy cradled and rocked him, apologizing and crying, while the sun crept lower in the sky and the east Texas woods grew dark and the wind out of the north picked up speed.

She laid the wet and mangled corpse on the ground and took off her jacket, sweatshirt, and T-shirt, then put her sweatshirt and jacket back on before she wrapped the cat in the T-shirt. She held him to her chest with her left arm, picked up the trap, and returned to her trailer where she dropped the trap and laid the cat on top of it. She took the shovel that leaned against the end of the trailer and dug a hole. It was only about a foot deep: the surface dirt was soft enough, but the underlying impacted sand was hard for Tammy to dig even when it was warm and her hand was uninjured.

She put the corpse, still wrapped in the blood-donation T-shirt, in the hole, raked the dirt back in, and placed a paving stone over it. She leaned the shovel back against the trailer and looked sorrowfully at the seven paving stones under the pine tree ten yards from the end of the trailer. She had accidentally killed one backing over it with her car, and had found five dead under the bridge.

"I'm so sorry!" she wailed.

Inside the trailer it was marginally warmer. The wind whistled outside, blowing underneath as well as around the shabby structure. Originally there had been skirting around the bottom, but she had removed it to keep critters from getting trapped there.

She sat on the pine folding chair at the table and dropped her face in her hands. They smelled of the creek. She clasped them in prayer.

"Lord," she said, "I'm sorry. I meant to help, and I didn't. I didn't help at all."

She tried to comfort herself with the thought of Jesus holding the cat, now warm and healthy and purring, but the image had become like a blanket that had been used and laundered too many times—it just had no comfort left to it.

"I can't do this anymore. I know it's what You want me to do, but I just can't do it anymore."

She leaned onto the table and fell asleep. She slept deeply enough that she wasn't disturbed by the sound of the car pulling off the road at the end of the bridge some hundred feet from the trailer; she didn't awaken when the door slammed. Somewhere in her dream she heard Jesus softly calling, "Here, kitty, kitty, kitty," but did not see His face.

While Tammy dreamt, Randy was opening three cans of cat food under the bridge near her trailer. He had ground the caplets into powder and stirred the powder into the pate.

He dropped dollops of the baited fare onto jar lids. "Lord, let it be quick and painless. Please forgive me; I know You will. This is what You want me to do."

The jar lids distributed on the shore below the bridge, Randy wiped his hands on his jeans, uncomfortable as Pilate. Then he got back into the aging Corolla and started the engine.

In Tammy's dream, Jesus cranked up the holy helicopter. When it woke her up, she thought she heard a car driving over the bridge. She was not sure. She went to the sink, washed her hands and face in painfully cold water, crawled under the Mexican blankets on the built-in sofa, and cried herself back to sleep.

> Listen to the top with the little birds singing
> And the melody and the high notes ringing
> The hoot-owl calls over everything
> And the blackbird disagrees

"Did you get the suet?"

Randy set the packages on the table and drew a deep, slow breath. He was determined to keep his temper, although sometimes his mother seemed determined to wrench it from him. Of course he had gotten the suet. That was what he had gone out for, and the packages were in his hands.

"Yes, Mother." His cheerful voice placated her. Placation. Hardly a relationship basis, but it was easier than arguing with the woman upon whose disability checks Randy—and the birds—depended.

She heaved herself out of the recliner and waddled into the kitchen. "Let me do it," she snapped. "You always make a mess."

As she heated and strained the suet, Randy took the bags of seed to the back porch and returned with the last of the older seed. He measured it out, then sat at the table to watch his mother turn the seed and suet into lumps of nutritious winter food for the wild birds, the songbirds the feral cats were killing.

Bobbette Parkins was amazingly deft in the kitchen for a five-foot, 280-pound woman with a bad back and arthritic hips and knees. Randy admired the way she handled utensils and ingredients: a Van Cliburn of the kitchen island. Sitting on the barstool at the island, he watched her, as he had since childhood, meld suet, peanut butter, and seeds for the birds the same way she melded meat, rice, and gravy for the two of them.

Bobbette banged the wooden spoon on the side of the pot, gratified by the approbation of her son—not her only one, but the only one who had stayed home.

"Just doing the Lord's work," she responded to his smile.

"Me, too."

She only had to make the stuff and could count on him to put it out for the birds. With her knees, it would have taken her hours to do what Randy could do in minutes. She shook her head; that was the cross the Lord had given her to bear.

"Did you put out the cat food last night?"

"Yes, ma'am."

She nodded. She was willing to pretend that cats were God's creatures too, but she knew for sure her precious birds were, and the birds belonged in these Piney Woods. The cats didn't.

"Was she there?"

"I didn't see her. There wasn't a light on at her place."

"Hmph."

"Mom, Tammy's just doing what she thinks is right."

Bobbette slammed the wooden spoon on the island beside the stovetop.

"Do *not* defend that woman!"

"I'm not! I'm not!"

"You are, too; you just did! Don't tell me you're not when you just did. I know her. She was my best friend!"

"Mom, come sit down. Come on."

Bobbette's color slowly returned from pale eggplant to pasty white as she pulled her arm from Randy's grasp. She breathed hard and wiped the sweat from her face.

"I'm fine. I gotta finish these."

She ladled the liquid mess into molds—the empty cat food cans Randy had brought back were a good size—and looked with satisfaction at the assorted shapes of hardening food. She nodded to Randy, who slid the baking sheet that held the cans into the refrigerator beside the jug of hummingbird nectar.

"The birds will love these."

"I hope so." Bobbette wiped the grease from her pudgy hands as she settled back in the recliner and handed the tea-towel to Randy.

"Put that in the laundry basket, will you? And tomorrow is Sunday."

"I know."

"You'll need to iron a shirt."

"I know, Mom. I will." He dropped the tea-towel on the mound of laundry and decided that, as long as he was being dutiful, he would be aggressively so. "I'll take this to the Laundromat."

Bobbette grunted and nodded as she picked up the television remote. For once, she hadn't had to insist he get the laundry done. She tried to pay attention to *America's Funniest Videos* but was distracted by thoughts of Tammy. She had loved having Tammy as a friend; they had met at choir practice, and Tammy had given her a magazine from the Audubon Society, which had educated her about the birds she loved—the songbirds of deep east Texas: mockingbirds that sang all night, finches, tanagers, orioles, the eastern bluebird, cardinals, ring-necked doves, ruby-throated hummingbirds—she loved them all, even the pigeons her daddy used to shoot, calling them rafter rats because they nested in the barn.

But Tammy was a cat person. She claimed she loved the birds, but how can someone love cats and birds at the same time? Feral cats killed millions of songbirds every year, and Tammy's solution was ridiculous: to trap cats, have the nasty things spayed or neutered, and release them where they had been trapped. While Bobbette acknowledged that neutering them kept them from reproducing—she wasn't stupid, after all —feral cats still savaged her birds. Right and left if you believed the brochures, and Bobbette did. And so she and Randy had started a campaign of their own.

The Tylenol with codeine, which had been prescribed for her hips, was sacrificed for the birds. Randy had mixed it into the cat food in the cans where the suet was now hardening, and the traces of Tylenol that remained would have the same effect on the birds as they did on the cats. It would take some up to five days to die.

Singing in the nighttime, singing in the day
The little duck quacks that he's on his way
The otter hasn't got much to say
And the porcupine talks to himself

Pastor Fortenberry didn't change into choir robes; he simply left the lectern at the end of his sermon and took his place in the left arm of the choir. His black robes set him apart a little, but since he was the pastor, it was all right to stand out.

Mrs. Murphy at the piano gave them their pitch; Bobbette had a soprano solo at the beginning and sang sweetly. The rest of the choir was about to join in when there was a disturbance among the altos. Half of the choir members persisted in the anthem; of the other half, some were knocked over by Tammy's fall, and others felt it inappropriate to keep singing when a woman had fallen down. Mrs. Murphy, her back to the choir, played a few bars past the point when the entire choir gave up before she joined the congregation in trying to see what had happened. In the choir and in the congregation, heads rose on necks until the Little Brown Church in the Vale looked as if it were home to a large gaggle of geese.

In the choir area, stage left from the altar, metal folding chairs were lined up on three levels. The men were lined up on the third row, basses left and tenors right. The front two rows were dedicated to the women, altos in front of the basses on both levels, and in front of the tenors second sopranos on the middle tier, and first sopranos on the front. Bobbette, as soloist, was on the far end. Between the awkward vantage point and her limited flexibility she couldn't see what had happened until a semi-circle of choir members slowly expanded from the center of the disturbance. In that center, a shoeless foot stuck out from a pile of choir robes.

"Tammy!" Bobbette cried out. "Randy, help her up! Help her!"

Randy struggled around the other tenors, finally stepping over the back of an upright metal folding chair, his weight tipping it and him over in his effort to get to Tammy, his music flying. The altos who could have helped break his fall pulled back as one body, and he sprawled on the floor at their feet. His elbows throbbing, he got onto his hands and knees beside Tammy, unconscious on the floor. Untrained in matters medical, he half-heartedly patted her hand and said her name in an effort to rouse her.

Bobbette stood above them, wringing her hands. "It's those cats! Those awful cats. She's got cat-scratch fever. I just know it!"

Pastor Fortenberry, uncertain whether cat-scratch fever was contagious, backed away from the scene, kindly pulling other basses away from the danger zone. To appear helpful, he scanned the congregation for Dr. Stanley, a retired veterinarian who was a sometime congregant, but didn't see him. He caught sight of Stella, who motioned him to get as far as possible from the threat; she was delicate and kept him and herself as far from sickness as she could; for her sake, he complied. Mrs. Murphy pulled her cell phone from her robes and dialed 911.

Pastor Fortenberry felt it prudent—or at least convenient—to dismiss the congregation with a final blessing and to ask them to leave in an orderly manner. Few left. It would be at least a half hour before the ambulance might arrive, so while the rest lingered to experience the end of the excitement, he retreated with Stella to his office to wait. And to pray for the poor woman. Mrs. Murphy stayed on her cell phone and gave Randy second-hand instructions to keep Tammy warm and still as she lay pale and shuddering among the upturned metal folding chairs.

Tammy would be treated successfully for Newcastle Disease, which she had caught from an infected oriole she had kept safe and fed in a box while its broken wing healed. It was Randy who had cat-scratch fever, but it was mild and went undiagnosed, as did Bobbette's chronic histoplasmosis from contact with bird feces.

Bobbette's birds would suffer a population drop as a result of the medication she had meant for Tammy's cats, and the relatively sudden death of so many birds created a West Nile virus scare that undermined tourism at the creek the following summer. Many put their cabins up for sale, but few buyers cared to take up residence there even after the assurance that it was not West Nile but an unaccountable wave of liver failure that had caused the drop in the bird population. People didn't seem to want to catch liver failure either.

The buck whose now-glass eyes kept vigil above the mantel of the parsonage was replaced as head of the herd by another buck. The deer population remained the same, even after Pastor Fortenberry relinquished his deer lease to the timber company that owned the land; they moved on to a neighboring forest when the trees were cut.

It's a simple song, a living song everywhere
By the ox and the fox and the grizzly bear
The grumpy alligator and the hawk above
The sly old weasel and the turtledove

Love at First Sight
by Grace Megnet

My old car was as good as dead, the mechanic said yesterday. He repaired the tie rod—I had understood thyroid—and then gave me the bad news. It felt like the tie rod problem had metastasized to the under-structure of my car.

"It's only a car," I said, but I was lying. Nobody, not even a cat or a dog, much less any one human knew my story as well as did that car. He —with my Germanic background I think of cars as male—was there from the beginning, or almost. The old Taurus, which friends let me use for free, knew about the first tears, the daily tears of the overwhelmed immigrant, overwhelmed by the number of toothpastes in the supermarket, over-whelmed by the acronymic gibberish in the staff meetings at St. Anthony's. I cried every day in that big, taupe Taurus. He was the car of tears, the place where I cried alone before I pasted on my brave smile and stepped into the world. Soon he had enough—it was a relationship of convenience from the start—and he stopped on the hightway at eighty-eight thousand. I left him there and walked away. What next? I did not like the cheap second-hand car which I could afford with the few thousand dollars I had saved so painfully for bad times.

"It's a bargain," the salesman raved. It belonged to an old lady who died." Exactly, that is how it felt, like putting on a pair of second-hand shoes where you can feel the hills and mounts of the former owner's footprint. I had enough of second-hand shoes and did not want a second-hand car for fear it came with a 50s hat with veil and faux pearls for Sunday church. It smelled like that, like a world where I did not belong. Across the parking lot I had spotted a small, black car.

"Totally out of your price range," the salesman sneered. But he looked cute. He blinked at me and pulled me over, and then, a test drive and we were in love, both happy to be alone with each other. I don't know how I found the money, but I cried less because he was mine. And he was there for me until he got sick and his tie rod metastasized. Early in our relationship he drove me to Houston, to art museums and calligraphy classes. Sometimes, when I had enough cash, we would stop at the Chinese supermarket. "That," I pointed to my favorite noodle dish, because they could not speak English either, and then ate the food out of a Styrofoam container in the parking lot. Once I figured out how to pump gas and pay with a credit card, he was easy on me. He didn't ask for much and not once anything but his standard drink, predictable, every 350 miles, 554 times. I hoped we would go to the moon together, but he got exhausted like my dad and quit too early, dependable and loyal to a fault, ready to roll, day and night. Every morning for work, at four o'clock on Thursdays to grad school through the Big Thicket listening patiently to the chatter with my friend Susan. Susan taught me the American life: Never admit to depression, not even on a job application, never. When we did not talk about art, about school, about Charlie or any of the other teachers, we talked about men. She talked about George and Fred, and I wanted to know how to find a George or a Fred.

"Men like long hair, and be careful. As soon as you spot a red flag, call it quits. Men want sex about three to four times a week."

She must know. I could tell. The A/C was his only weak point. That could have been a red flag, but I only discovered it in his later years. He got hot, but at least he did not yell or kick or beat. I had to open the window, and other people in old clunkers with open windows waved at me or talked to me at traffic lights.

The new car stands demure and a bit shy in the driveway. It is faster, jumpy and nervous like a teenager. The old car stands beaten, lusterless, worn, especially on the left side where the hot Texas sun ate the paint over the years. Like an old horse, he still has some life left. And what about the memories? He was the only one there, waiting for me patiently, when I came back from Europe—how many times—at midnight, jetlagged, and lonely.

"You can do it, you can do it, youcandoit," his engine hummed as we drove into the night, tired and alone. He drove me to the courthouse when I became a citizen; I finally also had an American number plate like him. A Japanese-American and a Swiss-American with an American-American cat living in an American-American house, a Texas house. He drove me to Houston on that sunny morning in April 2005 when I went to pick up that man from the internet. I parked him, the car, on the third floor of the parking garage and waited, waited for over an hour—I was nervous

—until he descended that staircase, in his blue Hawaiian shirt and black Dockers, exactly as he had told he would. I recognized him immediately. We tried to make small talk as we waited for the luggage.

"I can help you carry," I offered.

"No need," he said and smiled. We kissed in the car, and later talked and talked and talked.

We evacuated together, ran away from Rita. We could not go home for six weeks until the power was back on. It took so long because the utility trucks were all putting the power back in New Orleans. We saw them, the long lines of trucks coming from the entire continent. We evacuated for Gustav and for Ike. Ike was bad too, but I was not alone anymore because Francisco decided to stay, and life was different, better, good. He messed up the car with his black lab, but that was not important. The car was small, but that was not important either. He, the car, was still there waiting when we came back from our trips, but I was not sad anymore. There were arguments in the car sometimes, but never tears, and even when we drove into the night we drove home. With the new man came a new job. "You should get a new car," Francisco told me, but how could I throw him away? He who had seen my mom. She liked me to drive her around in my little black car over bayous and through rice fields. She liked drives along the gulf when the dunes were still there. We took the ferry at Bolivar and ate crawfish at Landry's. She liked crawfish. The new car will never see my mother. She is too old and does not fly anymore. We talk over the phone, and I should e-mail her a picture of my new car. It has all these buttons, electric this, power that, rear this, side that, even a vanity mirror and a sunglass compartment. It smells new as I look into the mirror —vainly—with my glasses and talk hands-free. It smells new and void. Void of memories.

The Guest
Jaya Wagle

Riddle me this: What do you do if you don't like the people you live with? In my case, it is my son, Suresh and his wife Tulsi. I live with them in a steel and glass house filled with modern furniture made of angular lines and hard surfaces. The walls are painted in shades of grey and brown, and food is served in white crockery that reminds me of a hospital.

I know my son asked me to stay with him out of a sense of obligation. I suppose I should be grateful. And I am. It's just that... you see living with my son is like living with a stranger. He left India when he was twenty-one to pursue his master's degree from Columbia University. In the last twenty years Suresh has been there, he has visited home twice: once for his wedding and the second time when his mother passed away.

The day after his mother's funeral, he said to me, "Papa, why don't you sell this big old house and come live with us in America?"

"What will I do there?" I said. "I don't know anyone there."

"You know me and Tulsi," he said.

But I *don't* know you and Tulsi, I wanted to say. Instead, I asked again, "What will I do there? Here, I have my routine."

"What routine?"

"Getting milk in the morning, going for a walk, reading newspaper, and watching soap operas, to name a few."

"You can do all that there too. I can't keep flying down here every time you get sick or something," he said. I wanted to ask him what he meant by "something" but decided not to.

I wasn't sure I wanted to sell my ancestral home to some real estate developer and move thousands of miles away with Suresh. But in the end, I agreed. I had always wanted to see America. I had heard so much about its skyscrapers and fast cars and loose women.

Before his mother fell ill from pneumonia she was making preparations to go visit Suresh. She was the one who got both our passports done and took care of the visas. Now that she is gone, I think her soul will rest in peace to know at least one of us is going to America.

It would have been different if she was here with me. Suresh was always closer to his mother than me. Not that I blame him. I was never the "involved father" like these younger generation boys are with their fancy strollers and baby carriers. In my time, it would have been considered outright laughable if not ridiculous to be so involved with your kids. The women folk took care of the house and the kids; men went out and earned a living. Life was simple. Our fruit basket had only fruits in it. My son's otherwise neat house has a big bowl on the kitchen counter that catches everything from stray fruit to cell phones and iPad chargers. Just looking at it drives me nuts, but I restrain myself. It is none of my business how they want to lead their lives, I reason.

My son helps his wife in the kitchen, they clean the house together, and I am sure when they have a kid, he will get up in the middle of the night to bottle-feed the crying infant. I mean what do you expect when they call each other *Sur* and *Taal* (Rhythm and Beat)? What is wrong with calling each other by their full names, Suresh and Tulsi? How hard is it to pronounce two more syllables?

Suresh is the proud owner of a fancy camera that he carries with him everywhere. Taal encourages him, pointing to all manner of objects to be photographed. I can't for the life of me figure out what the big deal is shooting a clump of fresh-pulled garlic bulbs or a zucchini crusted with dirt. Why go around taking pictures of vegetables and wasting reels of precious film?

"Papa, it is a digital camera. See, no photo reel," Suresh said. I peered into a small square at the back of the camera. It was focused on a rose. "I can shoot as many photos as I want, then select the ones I want to keep and delete the rest." Later, he pulled up hundreds of photos of food, flowers and plants on the computer screen.

"But what do you do with these pictures?" I asked, puzzled. I mean, it is not like the photos he was showing me were of giant tomatoes or funny shaped potatoes. They were just ordinary vegetables you could find at the farmer's market. Digital camera or not, I still didn't see the point of these photos.

Suresh went on to explain that he and Tulsi have a food blog. Not only do they post pictures of vegetables on it, they also post ("healthy") recipes and advise their followers on clean eating habits. It all made sense now. I realized why Taal spent so much time in front of the computer.

On my first day in their house, I couldn't find a drop of milk in the fridge.

"Papa, Taal is vegan," Sur said when I asked if they were out of milk.

"I thought vegetarians drink milk?" I asked, confused.

"No, Papa. There is a difference between vegetarians and vegans. Vegans don't consume any animal product, including milk," he said, and passed me a carton of soy milk. He explained how Taal was against exploiting animals for their milk, eggs, or meat. It was the strangest thing I had ever heard, but I kept my mouth shut. It was a good thing too because I soon realized that Sur and Taal experimented a lot with their diets.

There was the time when they went on an all fruit diet for a month. The house was filled with fruits of all kinds. They would make fruit salads and experiment with using fruit purees in desserts instead of real sugar and avocados instead of butter. I drank a lot of smoothies and ate a lot of pies during that phase.

I should have known the fruit diet was not going to last. One day Taal came home from the grocery store with milk, eggs, and something that looked like a cut-up chicken wrapped in clear plastic.

"We have decided to add milk and lean meats to our diets," she said, putting the milk carton in the fridge. Apparently, eating animal byproducts was okay as long as they were treated humanely, whatever that meant. This was good news for me, though. Now, I could have regular milk with my tea instead of that synthetic tasting soy milk. But Taal was not finished talking about the new diet.

"We did some research and realized that whole grains are bad for you. From now on, no more oatmeal, whole wheat or grains of any kind," she said with that annoying know-it-all shake of her head.

So far, their crazy diets had made me change and adjust my eating habits every few months. The smoothies were okay, and some were even delicious. I detested soy milk and was drinking black tea for the last few months. The oatmeal and the *rotis* were the only two constants from my Indian diet that had been left untouched. Now they wanted to take it away from me for some newfangled study that said whole grains were not good for you. I never heard such baloney in all my sixty-nine years. These two need to lighten up on their diet and work up an appetite on making a baby.

But I dare not bring up the subject lest they have some theory about that too. I can just picture Sur telling me, "There are too many orphans in this world for us to reproduce a child and overburden the earth."

But, then again, what do I know? I am an invisible man. It didn't matter what I thought, and I did not have the strength or the paternal love to argue their flawed logic. If they wanted to eat meat, eggs and vegetables and forgo whole grains, it was their choice. All I cared about were my two *rotis* in the morning and my rice at night.

"Believe me, Papa, you will feel better, and your body will thank you for not eating all that grain." Taal tried to explain her nutrition jargon like I was a five-year-old child.

After that lecture, Taal declared that all the flours and whole grains had to be thrown out to minimize temptation and craving. I sat on the steel dining room chair, the cold seeping through my pants, and watched as the two raided the pantry and started throwing out packets of flour and emptying oatmeal containers into a garbage bag. Back home, the maid would have gladly taken all that food and fed her children. But in the land of plenty, one did not give open groceries to the less fortunate.

Around the time whole-grains were banished from the house, the weather turned. The barren trees started sprouting leaves and flowers. The sun was out longer, and the days were longer. I started going on walks around the neighborhood. One morning, I missed a turn and ended up on a street that didn't have an exit. I am told it is called a cul-de-sac. I was retracing my steps back when I saw her in a window, reading a book. A steaming cup of chai rested on the windowsill. She looked Indian and had a comely face, unlike the thin-lipped face of Taal. She probably eats whole grains as well as fruits and milk and eggs, I thought.

One evening, after a particularly monotonous day at the house, I decided to walk up to her front door and ring the bell. It was late in the evening, and I wasn't even sure what I was doing there. Her husband opened the door with the manner of someone expecting company. He seemed like a decent-enough fellow.

"Yes, can I help you?" he asked.

"*Beta*, I take a walk every day . . ." I began, unsure of where I was going with this.

"Are you lost, uncle?" he asked me.

"Yes." This was perfect. It was logical for an old man to get lost.

"Do you have your family's number? I can call them for you."

This was a problem for me. If I gave him Suresh's number, he may not like that I had veered off his carefully planned route or troubled a stranger. "That's why I asked you to stay on the path, Papa," I could hear him say.

"I don't have my son's number with me today, but if you point me to the fountain, I know my way from there," I said. It was partially true. Suresh's house was across from the fountain.

"Why don't you come in and have a glass of water? I can drop you to the fountain as soon as my wife comes out of the shower," he said.

This was better than I expected. I followed him into a large living room with comfortable sofas and chairs filled with cushions. One wall was painted a bright orange, and the rest of the walls were a sunny, golden yellow.

"I'll check if my wife is done getting ready, and then I'll drop you by the fountain," he said, going around a corner of the room.

He soon came back with the girl I had seen in the window. Her name was Naina and his was Ajay. She was dressed in a *salwar kameez* and was very polite. She said they were expecting company and went into the kitchen. I could smell the heady, pungent aromas of garam masala and crackling mustard seeds. I detected the woody smell of okra fry, and my mouth watered. It was one of my favorite vegetables, but in my son's carb-free house okra was a vegetable neither Sur nor Taal liked.

I would have taken them up on their offer to stay for dinner, but my pager started vibrating, and I knew I had to head back home. The pager was my son's way of keeping tabs on me, making sure I did not wander off or get lost in the cookie-cutter houses and lanes of this community. Ajay walked out with me and guided me to the fountain.

I went back home that day and had some steamed vegetables and a piece of chicken seasoned with salt and pepper for dinner. Taal didn't care to cook traditional Indian food. "The smell of spices clings to the carpet and clothes," she said. At the end of the meal, she took some brownies from the fridge and put them in front of me.

"These are very nutritious," she said. "They are made with dark chocolate and nuts and dates mixed together."

They looked delicious, and I took a big bite. I almost gagged at the bitterness. "*Beti*, did you forget to put sugar in them?" I asked.

"Papa, sugar is not good for the human body. I sweetened the brownies with raisins and date puree. Eat some more; you will get used to the bitterness, and after a while you won't even miss the sugar." Sur looked at Taal adoringly as she explained to me, once again, the benefits of a sugar-free diet.

I nodded and waited for them to go to bed before I took out my secret jar of honey. An instinct, born out of the previous diet phases, had made me hide the jar inside an empty Quaker Oats container and keep it under the sink. I took a small bowl from the cabinet, poured some honey in it, and dipped the brownie in the golden liquid and took a sugary, sweet bite.

Tomorrow, I will go over to Naina's house around lunchtime. Hope she is making okra fry again. I just might stay for lunch if she asks.

Nails on the Blackboard
Caroline Watanabe

The smell of burnt coffee and stale air filled my nose as I entered the small room. I could almost taste the bitter black coffee in the hands of the couple already seated and comfortable. This was the first time I had seen the room occupied. I felt the excitement of what I was finally about to witness. I had spent days warming up to copy machines, filing, and alphabetizing for my boss. I was glad to take a break from that and sit in on one of the interviews everyone keeps talking about.

The large man with white whiskers sat near the door I walked in. He was in business casual attire. I noticed his weapon holstered on his right hip. He was asking the young woman sitting across from him a favor.

"The grape one, if you can find it."

"There's only cherry."

"Damn it. Need to tell Shannon to refill that."

"Still want something?"

"Humph. Just grab me a Tootsie Roll."

"Here you go, O'Conner."

The lady chuckled and grabbed the cherry sucker for herself and looked up to me.

"Are you sitting with us for this one? I saw you in the lobby and was wondering who you were. My name is Joy. I'm with Child Protective Services."

She smiled and held out her hand. I immediately noticed her swollen midriff. Her pregnant stomach did not match her business attire.

"Hi, nice to meet you. I'm Emma, the intern."

The whiskered man added, "Oh, sorry, I'm detective O'Conner. Here as an intern, eh? I remember when I was a rookie. Glad those days are gone."

Yes, I get the grunt work. But not today, I thought, seating myself between them in the black leather chair. It tilted ever so slightly backwards when I leaned back. I was somewhat jealous of O'Conner and Joy who got to sit in chairs for hours. This was a luxury for me. I had gotten used to hard uncomfortable wooden chairs and working on my feet.

"'Bout to retire now, though," O'Conner said with a relieved sigh.

"How long have you worked here?" I asked.

"I've worked for the police for over forty years. Joined fresh out of college."

This man has worked for two of my lifetimes, I thought. I suddenly felt very young working alongside someone who has seen so much.

"Have you always worked with cases like this?" I asked.

"No, I started about ten years ago. It's tough work but worth it."

"Well, congratulations on your retirement. Can't say any of us will miss you here," Joy teased with a wink. I noticed the wrinkles around her eyes that she attempted to cover with make-up. I did not think she was very old, but her face looked tired and worn out.

"So how many months?" I asked, eyeing Joy's stomach.

"Five and counting. It's been rough. I've had to skip a couple of days of work. I hate doing that. Plus my ex keeps calling me up, so that doesn't make things easier."

"Boys are always trouble, I tell you. Get rid of the rotten ones when you can," O'Conner chimed in.

"Is this your first pregnancy? Is it a boy or girl?" I hoped I wasn't asking for too much information.

"No, I have a son. This one's with my second husband. It's a girl."

"You better watch those kids," O'Conner said.

"Oh, believe me I do, and I will."

The temperature rose with another body in the little room. Though the metallic blinds shut out the August sun, I could feel warmth radiating from the windowsill. The low hum from the recording devices filled the lulls of our conversation. I examined the room, but there was nothing that greatly attracted my attention. The walls were off-white and bare. Tack holes dotted some parts of the wall. The plain gray carpet looked new, but it already had a coffee stain near my feet. The wall we faced hid behind several heavy duty pieces of devices used to record the interviews conducted in the room next door. A small TV screen sat on the desk with two large speakers on each side with live-feed from the hidden camera in the interview room. A thin layer of gray dust shrouded the tops of the equipment with the exception of a small area on a black metal drawer near Joy where the cup of candy sat. The heat was starting to get more noticeable. The bottom of my thighs began to stick to the leather padding on my chair.

"So what made you want to come into our cave of pedophiles and perves? School? I'm sure it's put a damper on your summer," Joy asked.

"I needed to get an internship, and I happened to come across the advocacy center. And I wanted to be able to help out in our community," I answered.

To be honest, this was an internship that began as an excuse to get out of the house during the summer. It turned out to be a great opportunity for me as a psychology major interested in social work. The job soon pulled me into a world of crises, but I enjoyed the work for the most part.

"I understand," Joy smiled, tired.

"Sometimes you need more than good intentions, though. This is real work," grunted O'Conner, without looking at me.

Silence ensued. I readjusted myself awkwardly in the chair.

"So what's the case today?" I asked.

"We got a call from a teacher at the local school the day before last. One of her students said she was raped by a family friend," the detective said, preparing his notepad.

"Did her parents come with her then?" I asked.

"No, the teacher. The mom was busy. I think her aunt is on her way."

The door clicked open, and I turned toward the door, but no one came in. I realized it was the sound coming from the speakers on the TV as it came to life. The interview room was spacious and had one table and two chairs. A girl slumped into one of the chairs.

The door to our room opened abruptly, and a middle-aged woman walked in. The cooler air rushed in from the hallway. Shannon was the head of the interviewers, and my boss. I found myself straightening my back.

"God, it's so hot in here. The air never works right in this room."

"Tell me about it. And where are my damn grape suckers?" O'Conner asked.

"We like to torture our detectives," Shannon winked and asked me, "Are you ready for your first observation, Emma?"

I nodded.

"This will be a good one to watch. And I told Jessica to have you

118

observe her filling out paperwork with the family after this," she said and turned to O'Conner.

"Have you met the girl?" Shannon lowered her voice.

"Yeah. I know it'll be interesting."

"Tell me about it."

"Do you think she'll talk?"

"Not sure. I think so. What do you think of this case?"

"As long as she doesn't say anything stupid and make shit up like the last one, I'll be happy," O'Conner said.

Shannon put a blank DVD into one of the recorders but did not start recording. She left the room as abruptly as she came in. I saw her reappear on the small screen.

Shannon informed the girl about the hidden camera and the microphone. I was hoping to get a look at the girl's face, but she remained still, her black hair covering her face.

"Shannon is one of the best we've got," O'Conner said to me, without taking his eyes off the screen. "If you want to learn how to do this, learn it from her."

"I'll be asking you many questions," Shannon's voice echoed in the speakers. "We're recording this so that you don't have to tell this story over and over again."

The girl adjusted herself. She sat on the edge of the chair, both hands under the table. She was tense and looked eager to leave. Shannon asked if she was ready for this. The girl shrugged.

Shannon came into our room again and clicked the button to start recording.

"Well, this may end up being a short interview," Shannon said, leaving.

"Let's get going. I want to have lunch with my wife today," O'Conner checked his watch.

"Do you know the perpetrator?" Joy asked O'Conner. "I heard he was quite a catch."

"Yeah. Adrian caused us trouble before with girls her age and was apparently her mother's frequent customer."

Joy winced.

"How old is he anyway?"

"Twenty-five."

"I was informed that the mother had two kids. Where's the other one?"

"The son is in prison for drugs. He didn't know anything about Adrian. Not surprising."

"And the Dad?"

"A drunk. Last time I checked he was doing time too."

"Can't say I don't know how that feels. That's too bad," Joy shrugged.

I wished they would stop talking. I wanted to listen to what the girl was saying. They probably knew where the cruxes were in the interview, but I wanted to soak in every detail. I could barely hear Shannon's voice, and the girl's soft voice was even harder to hear over the high pitched voice of Joy and the gruff voice of O'Conner. I never took my eyes off the girl on the screen.

"Do you know why you are here today?" Shannon asked.

"I think so," the girl said. I thought I heard an accent. Joy and O'Conner finally quieted down.

"Can you tell us more about that?"

The girl began to defend her friends at school, how they were not a bad influence, and that they did not actually smoke pot. Her mother had accused them falsely, the girl said. Her mother did not like her friends.

"It's okay, we're not out to get your buddies about that," Joy said.

"Maybe. I'm going to check on that later, to be sure. She never talked to me this much. I swear girls just open up better to other girls," O'Conner added.

"Well, that's because when you ask questions, you look scary as hell," Joy laughed.

I could imagine O'Conner being a strict officer. The creases on his forehead told of many frowns.

"Let's just hope she doesn't bullshit us like the last one did. That just pisses me off," O'Conner said. "Cops aren't dumb."

"Why did your mom leave?" I heard Shannon's voice clearly.

"We had a fight."

"Can you tell me more about that?"

"There's this girl I like at school. She doesn't like that."

O'Conner sat up to write something in his notes. It was like watching and critiquing a movie. I had to pause and tell myself this girl in the screen was real. She was in the room next door. I felt a vibration. Joy fumbled around in her red purse and pulled out her phone. She smiled at the text. I guessed it was her current husband.

"Then what happened?" Shannon asked.

"Mom left. And Adrian came in the apartment awhile later."

"How did he come in?"

"Through the door, obviously."

"Does he have a key?"

"No. Mom usually keeps it open for her guys."

"Do you know him?"

"Yeah. He chills with Mom a lot. He knows some of my friends too. He buys us dinner sometimes. He's nice for the most part. He said he wanted to play with me. But I didn't want to."

"What do you mean by 'play'?"

"He wanted me to take off my clothes."

"Have you played this game with him before?"

"Sometimes."

O'Conner and Joy groaned.

"Tell me more about what happened that night when your mother left."

Anticipation shot through our room as we waited for her answer. I had an idea of what she was going to say, but I wanted to know for sure. I wanted to hear it from her.

"He came in the house and just sat on our couch and stared at me. I told him to leave me alone, but he wouldn't leave. I told him Mom would be back soon, but he just kept staring. It was really creepy. I went into my room and shut the door and tried to do some homework. He came in my bedroom and told me to never talk to him like that."

The girl's voice had been steady all along, but it began to waver. She whispered, and we all leaned closer to the speakers. We could barely hear her.

"Damnit girl, speak up; this is important," O'Conner snapped.

"You can do this," Joy said. I wondered who they were really talking to.

The girl further sank into her chair and recounted to us what Adrian had done. Her posture made me think of a child cowering in shame after losing something dear to her. But there was no need to be sorry, I thought. It wasn't her fault, but did she know it? Her fingers uncomfortably scratched her thighs. I wondered if she was reliving the incident, perhaps trying to scratch away the memory on her skin of his violent touch. She tried to pull her skirt down. It was too short. She looked like a child to me.

"How long did he stay for?"

"I don't remember. It felt like a couple of hours."

"The nurse did mention some scarring," Joy murmured almost to herself as she traced her bulge with her fingers.

Together, we sat there in the room and listened to her cry.

Shannon paused and let the girl sob for a minute or two. All I heard was her amplified whimpering from the speakers. I felt like an intruder witnessing something I was not supposed to see. I turned away from the screen, though it did not make a difference. She did not even know I was there, hanging on her every word. A small lens separated us, preventing any form of contact or comfort. Her whimpers came across to me like nails on a blackboard and were seared on my memory. She knew me not.

"Did your mom come back?"

"No. She went to stay at a friend's house. I called her to tell her what happened."

"What did she do?"

"Nothing. Said I was being whiny and didn't believe me at first. But then she said..."

There was a long pause. I almost thought I just missed what she said.

"What did she say?"

"She said...that I deserved it."

The detective raised his eyebrows, and Joy scribbled something down on her notes.

I tried to think of my mother saying those words to me, but I could not. The back of my eyes stung. I was afraid to be the only one struck by her mother's words. I turned my eyes toward Joy, measuring her response. She was texting again while she continually stroked her belly. My struggle to stay tearless managed to go unnoticed.

O'Conner began his commentary again: "We're not the shrink. Come on, get it out. We all want this over too."

"Did you catch the guy?" I asked.

"Yeah, we got him. He ain't gonna be touching any of those girls for a long time."

"So what's going to happen?"

"We'll use this girl's testimony to lock him up for as long as we can. There were others too, but hers would be crucial. It'll depend on the jury, but we got this guy good, I think," O'Conner said.

"It's still hard to say now, Emma. O'Conner and I will be working on this case for a while, but really nothing is for certain until he's behind bars for good. Even then...knowing her lifestyle, there's a high chance this may not even be the first or last time for this kind of thing to happen to her."

"Gotta pick your battles, or you won't win any."

This was the tip of the iceberg, but they had to start somewhere. I wondered how many cases failed to even get to court. I looked at the girl. Will she also slip through the cracks of this system?

"Is this the only time this has happened?" Shannon continued.

"Please say yes," O'Conner mumbled.

"Mhm."

Sighs gave out from O'Conner and Joy. Less paperwork and less time in this sauna—I could just hear their thoughts. Shannon also asked about her sexual history.

"Have you been sexually active?"

"I wouldn't be surprised," huffed O'Conner.

"No," the girl said.

O'Conner grunted.

"What? That's bullshit," Joy snapped, "I swear she told me something else when we talked before this."

"Has anyone tried to play these games with you before?" Shannon asked.

O'Conner prepared to write down names.

"No."

O'Conner grunted again. Joy was still mumbling to herself in frustration.

Shannon began to ask questions on a lighter and casual note. It sounded like she was wrapping up.

"Well, I'm going to leave you for a second to check on how the video recording is going."

Shannon walked back into our room.

"Did I hit everything you wanted?"

"Yup. You read my mind. Thanks," said O'Conner, putting up his notes.

"I swear, she told me something else when I talked to her yesterday" Joy said, looking at the girl on the TV screen.

"You get what you get," O'Conner said, sighing.

Shannon went back to inform the girl the interview was over, and she may return to the waiting room when she's ready.

Jessica walked in and informed me that the girl's aunt would arrive in half an hour, and that she was expecting me to be there to meet the aunt in the family room. There, I was to watch another part of the process unfold.

"Meanwhile, go take your break," Jessica said, leaving.

I stood up and left our little room.

My mind was elsewhere, thinking back on the girl and her tears and the reactions from O'Conner and Joy. I wasn't sure what to feel, or what I should feel. I wanted a cold drink. As I was fumbling for my car keys, I walked straight into the girl coming out of the interview room. My sweaty arms recoiled reflexively at the touch of her cool skin. She was about my height, on the shorter side. If she straightened her back, she might have been an inch or two taller than me. Her dark caramel skin was contrasted with the white see-through shirt and blue jean skirt hugging her hips. Her eyes were narrow, swollen, and red. She was heavyset despite her small frame. She looked much younger than the ripe age of sixteen.

When my eyes met her black almonds, I did not know what she saw. I hoped she saw some form of sympathy I tried to convey in the split second we collided, yet the way she looked at me made me doubt it. I feared her impression of me. She scrutinized my countenance, my clothes, and my slender frame. Her sharp gaze resented my approach, resenting me. I stepped back and managed to let out an "I'm sorry," but she had already walked off.

I turned the corner of the hall to escape from this building. I pushed open the emergency exit door leading to the parking lot in the back. The sudden sunlight was blinding. The blistering panhandle Texas air choked me. I hopped into my Cadillac and drove to the nearest coffee shop to get myself a cold frappe. I did not feel like waiting for the drive-thru, so I parked the car and walked in. I felt out of place with my professional dress amidst the bored teens and middle aged women gossiping around tables. I must have drawn some attention to myself because the young man taking my order kept smiling at me. I gave a faint smile back, but felt self-conscious. I checked myself to make sure I was not giving off any mixed signals, wondering what he thought of me. I fumbled for my change as he made my drink. I walked out of the coffee shop with a large frappe with his name and number written on the side. I questioned his intentions for doing so, and I threw the container away as soon as I finished it.

I got back just in time. I entered the family room where Jessica and the aunt sat around a round wooden table. This room was brighter and less stuffy. The cool air was a welcome relief to my sweaty skin. The blinds were open, revealing the great August sky. Its beauty was almost enough to keep my thoughts away from the girl.

I quietly sat down next to Jessica, tucking myself into the chair. The aunt filled out paperwork as Jessica pointed out the areas to fill out. I observed on the paperwork that the aunt's name was Nadia.

"I just don't understand her..." Nadia said and abruptly stopped her pen. "I never really liked my sister-in-law, but this?"

Jessica and I listened.

"A woman of that profession should not be raising children. She was always a terrible mother. I told Maggie she's welcome in my home any time, but her mother and I have never really gotten along. Maggie comes to me crying from fights with her mother. Every time it's something different. Maggie can't be perfect; I don't expect my children to be. She calls Maggie names I don't want to repeat. Disgusting words. And not even coming here to support her today? She is my niece, this is the least I can do, but I wish I could do more."

"I'm sure Maggie knows that you support her and your doors are always open," Jessica said softly. Those words that meant to comfort sounded rehearsed to me.

"I know...I just wish I could kidnap her to live with me. Maggie has no business living with that whore. I don't care if you have a daughter that's unattractive, bi-sexual, fat or even retarded. That's her daughter, for God's sake. She has no right to treat her daughter like that. I mean, she said *this* was Maggie's fault. This is her *baby* we're talking about. But I guess to some people that doesn't mean anything."

I gave out a sigh, glad to know there was someone that could look after Maggie. Nadia continued.

"And when the cop told me he may have been there for a couple of hours with no one to call for help? I might have died. Did Maggie say anything about that in the interview?"

Nadia looked straight at me. I immediately turned to Jessica.

"I'm sorry, we're not allowed to disclose that information. And I wasn't there listening to the interview, so I don't know what happened."

But Nadia was not listening. She clenched her pen and stared blankly at the paper in front of her. I followed her gaze to the paperwork. It was an application to be reimbursed by the local government for any monetary costs incurred from criminal victimization. It also potentially paid for counseling services if they were advised. It was almost comical to me to see how even in the most emotionally draining circumstances, money managed to poke its ugly head out to pester those in distress. It was almost a sick reminder for the families that their emotional pains were translated into monetary terms by the government. Nadia was filling out these forms in the place of Maggie's mother.

"This is how I see it, and it has helped me when working with cases like these," Jessica started. "If the child had the courage to tell us the truth, I feel it my duty to not let them down and do my job right, whatever that may be. Because that's the least I can do."

"Yeah, you're right... But that woman should be locked in jail with that bastard," she growled and began to choke up. "I just feel so helpless. Can't I do more?"

Nadia began to sob, like the girl on the screen.

I glanced sideways at Jessica. Her face was empathetic, but I felt there was still a layer of emotion hardened by years of practice and training. I had no layer. I was raw, vulnerable to feelings. I pretended to scratch my nose as I quickly wiped away a tear that had fallen out of place. I felt this woman's tears to be the only genuine expression in this room. My heart was slowly numbing, but it still ached to feel.

I handed her some Kleenex, wishing it was something more. Several minutes passed in silence. The aunt finished the paperwork while blowing her nose and wiping away her tears that never seemed to stop flowing.

"Did I fill out everything right?"

"Yes, ma'am. You're good with us here. I'll let you collect yourself before going back to Maggie. She's waiting for you in the lobby." Jessica got up to leave.

"Okay, thank you so much. I don't know how you guys do this. Thank you..."

No, thank *you*, I wanted to add. I stood up and left with Jessica, but not before one last glance at the aunt who was slouched over the table, her face in her hands, trembling. I was glad to have met her. I was thankful for her presence in Maggie's life. I wanted to touch her shoulder, her arm, her back, anything to encourage her and communicate my gratitude, but I could not. I felt insufficient and unworthy to offer that touch.

I got busy with helping the social workers organize some paperwork again. O'Conner left to go have lunch with his wife, and Joy hung around for a while talking to Jessica. Shannon was in the interview room again, with another child.

All the while I thought of ways to communicate in a small way that I feel for Maggie, for Nadia, and for this whole situation. But words of hope and sympathy coming from me sounded superficial and died on my lips. I felt my own failure to be the one that serves. I thought of offering them a drink to take with them, or a snack for the road back home, anything to release myself from the anguish of helplessness.

I went back into the lobby with a couple of Cokes in my hand, just in time to see Maggie and Nadia reunite. I saw them talk to each other, embrace, and even smile. The smile on Maggie's face lit up her dark eyes. She looked like a different person in that moment. She looked strong, young, and innocent. It was the most beautiful thing I saw that day, a smile that had every right to be extinguished forever. But there it was.

I put the drinks down on the table to give to the next family, who had just arrived.

This was the first and last day that I saw a piece of Maggie's broken life. Yet without forgetting her tears, I would remember her with that smile. As I observed more interviews and remained behind hidden cameras in the heat of crisis, I clung onto her smile as a beacon of my hope.

Hexed
Alikay Wood

It started with a note on the condom wrapper Shannon McClellan's boyfriend discarded on the floor when he snuck out of her room. She was shocked. Rob was not the romantic note type. But she could not deny the evidence before her in neat handwriting with an elegantly, humble finish.

Broan Lake
Midnight
Come or be hexed

The straightforward, no-nonsense tone meant it could be Rob. Although Shannon's friends had claimed his late night disappearances and flings with other women were sure signs of his promiscuous nature, she had always known better. He was probably going to propose. How sweet of him.

Jennifer White found a similar message written in lipstick on her mirror. Lauren Gilgor's was attached to an A- essay she was contesting with a professor. Perhaps most fantastically of all, Tara Blake found her invitation written in Sharpie on her own body. She was so hungover from the night before that she arrived at the lake late, having only awoken from her inebriated bliss with enough consciousness to examine her body and find the directions ten minutes earlier.

Six girls were waiting by the lake when Tara arrived. Lee Sun and Jennifer Johnson were resting on the hood of Jennifer's bubblegum pink convertible. Lee's head was engulfed by large padded headphones that did little to dull the brightness of her obnoxiously orange hair as it shook in time with an invisible song. Jennifer Johnson was small, perpetually anxious, and usually covered in hives. A secret midnight meeting at the lake at midnight with strangers, one of whom was the notoriously greasy slut Tara Blake, was only intensifying the clammy texture of her already porous skin.

The seven girls stood in a lopsided circle beside the small body of water, casting cautious looks at the others.

"So we all got the same message, I assume." Jennifer White stooped to pick up a pebble from the rocky beach. She skipped it into the muddy water and waited.

Shannon stared at the girl. She knew Jennifer from her Economics class and could not believe she was Rob's type. Rob liked lithe and limber, not independent and irrational. Jennifer White's squat, muscular body was incomparable to her own glossed, lust-inducing machine.

"What do you think it's for?" Brittany Spole asked as she swung her shin-guard-clad-legs back and forth, fumigating the air with her sweat-soaked socks.

"Wait, are all of you dating Rob?" Shannon asked.

"Don't be ignorant, Shannon," Lauren said. They had gone to the same high school and so she was well aware of Shannon's long history with obtuseness. "This is bigger than your libido."

"Who's Rob?" Lee asked in a forced American accent. No one answered. They were too preoccupied with the nymph of a girl who had suddenly placed herself in the middle of the circle. More interesting than how the girl had materialized without anyone noticing was the girl herself. Everything about her was a bizarre contrast of small and large. She was short with a head that reminded Brittany of a soccer ball and a concrete nose whose thickness could only be explained away with fantastical stories of extreme breaks and dense cartilage. Her hair fell down her back in sheen of brown and the moonlight cast her protruding cheekbones in an unforgiving light.

"My name is Mildred," she said, and the steadiness of her voice left no question as to her authority. "I'm here to guide you through the oldest and most important tradition in the history of Westbrook Preparatory School."

Mildred stood motionless in the center, hands clasped behind her back while her eyes penetrated each of their pupils with a focus so relentless it must have been rehearsed. Six headlights clicked on and flooded her with light simultaneously.

"There's someone out there?" Lauren asked.

"We are not alone," Lee said. Lee was very into science fiction, and the eeriness of the situation excited her immensely.

"You're here because you have been chosen. Each year six girls are selected. Each year six girls become one of us," Mildred continued, her body covered in cold, fluorescent light.

From outside the circle a quiet chanting began, its intensity only made fiercer by the restrained volume.

Hex. Hex. Hex. Hex.

The girls were still, each a statue cast in a unique position of unease, but their minds were reaching the same conclusion. It made sense that they were not alone. After all, secret societies had to have members to function.

"For almost two-hundred years, Hex has been the best kept secret of Westbrook. Our most prestigious and infamous alumni have stood in this very circle, faced with the same decision before you now. Choose carefully for it is a decision that will determine the path you walk from now on." Mildred paused, and the headlights flickered on and off. "If you would like to become a member step forward and state your name."

"Lauren Gilgor," was heard first, followed by Jennifer White, Lee Sun, Shannon Mclellan, Tara Blake, and Brittany Spole. Jennifer Johnson was the last to gather her courage and step forward into the artificial circle of light beaming from the trucks.

"Jennifer Johnson."

"Who the hell are you?" A faceless voice interjected from outside the circle of light.

"Uh," she hesitated, "Jennifer Johnson?"

"Were you invited to this gathering?"

"Yes, actually I was, um there was—"

"Don't waste my time."

"There was a note on one of my pill bottles," Jennifer finally managed to get out. Mildred considered the shaking girl before her and smiled.

"So there are seven of you now. Never mind, in a week there will be six." She turned toward Jennifer Johnson. "What's your name again?"

"Jennifer."

"Isn't she Jennifer?" Mildred pointed toward Jennifer White.

"Yes."

"So that would make you Other Jennifer."

"Well, actually, my middle name is April."

"Do not speak unless directed to, Other Jennifer."

Other Jennifer opened her mouth to speak, thought better of it and instead stepped back to join the relative safety of the circle. Mildred clasped her hands in front of her stomach, arched her back and strode out of the circle.

They followed because they did not know where she was going. They followed because nothing exciting ever happened in Westbrook. They followed because they did not want to be left alone. They followed because they were afraid.

Mildred came to a stop in front of a monstrously large black pick-up truck. "Get in the bed. Lay down. Don't talk."

Hands pulled hoods over their heads, and other hands yanked them up into the vehicle. Their feet landed in a thick, oozy liquid that smelled of ash, tar, and excrement.

"What is this?" Lauren asked.

"No questions," a voice that was not Mildred's responded.

"Do not grab onto anything. If you fall, stay down." That was Mildred. They heard a ballerina thump as she leaped to the ground.

Then the truck began moving.

Tara was the first to fall when the truck lurched forward. Her body slushed through the mystery liquid and collided with the ribbed bottom. She took Lee Sun down with her, and when she emerged ready to scream and throw herself overboard, it was Other Jennifer who delivered a silencing hand to the mouth.

"For generations each Hex has endured the exact same activities that you will endure tonight," Mildred shouted over the rumbling of the engine.

Lauren doubted they had ridden in the back of trucks in the mid 1800s, but she was too focused on survival to point this out.

"You will be tested." Mildred spit the last word from somewhere behind the truck, her saliva mingling with the mystery sludge coating the truck. "But have courage, friends. Gain strength in knowing that we have walked this path before you."

Tara, who was still slightly drunk from the night before, spoke to herself quietly, "I am special. I am chosen. I am special. I am chosen."

Jennifer White (not to be confused with Other Jennifer) picked it up next, until they were all whispering the words as their faces fell into the muck. It was surfing on sewage until no one could stand, and they were all one tangle of limbs, tumbling together through the mud and the filth. It went on until their teeth ached from clattering against each other; only when the shaking of their bodies had reached an audible level did Mildred's voice cut through the humming of the motor.

"Stand up." The truck stopped. She held out her hand and let her own creamy skin be defiled with their waste and smell, helping each of them to the ground. They were greeted by the sight of a bonfire and buckets of warm water to rinse themselves off. It was a chance to wash away their doubts and burn into them something else entirely. Allegiance.

"I'm proud of you," Mildred said. "We have all stood in that spot, we have all endured, and we are all more because of it." Her voice plied and massaged their questions straight out of their heads. "But this was only the beginning. Your second task is far more important. Tomorrow by 5 a.m., you will have dyed Lakewood Pond."

Jennifer White smiled. Brittany flexed her fingers at her sides. Lee was cleaning sludge off of her headphones with her hair. Shannon started crying. Lauren rolled her eyes. Tara slapped herself to make sure she'd heard correctly. Other Jennifer didn't move at all.

"Are you guys the ones who do the lake every year?" Shannon asked. Other Jennifer looked around nervously as if just mentioning the dying of Lakewood Pond would send administration scurrying.

"Oh, Shannon," Mildred said, making her way around the fire to pat her primly on the head. "It's *always* us."

"But how?" Lauren sputtered.

"You have four hours until the Headmaster wakes up," Mildred responded. "No one in the history of Hex has gotten caught." She climbed onto the bed of one of the clean trucks surrounding the fire and held on as it swerved forward in the direction of the highway. "Do not be the first."

* * *

So it was that six girls and one accidental invite found themselves shivering on the edge of a manmade lake, lugging buckets of food coloring and skinny brooms toward its shores. They examined the small pond, their eyes lingering on the reflection of the Headmaster's tower that fell across the middle of the lake while their hopes of becoming members of an elite secret society, for which they had been specifically chosen, dwindled.

"Do it, Lee," Brittany whispered, her voice captured immediately by the wind.

"Aw-right, aw-right." Lee waded into the water, trailing a bucket of liquid dye into the water behind her. "Lee take care for you."

Her pale skin stood out against the murky water, but despite the cold she didn't shake in the wind or wince at the rocks beneath her feet.

"Okay, let's go," Jennifer White said. The others waded in with large brooms and began circulating the color, Lauren letting out a series of neanderthal-esque grunts as they went.

Other Jennifer stood silently on the shore for a moment before plunging in, rotating her broom in large circles and spreading the yellow around the pond.

"Atta girl, Other Jennifer," Brittany said.

"You don't have to call her that. No one's here," Shannon said.

"It's practical," Jennifer White answered. "And you don't mind, do you?"

"Shut up; a light's coming on!" Tara said in a slurred voice. Somehow she had managed to consume a water bottle that was (unsurprisingly) not filled with water, during the short ride from the lake back to campus. It could be considered impressive if it weren't also pathetic.

"What do we do?" Other Jennifer asked, because sure enough a hollow candlelight was flickering in the curved window of the turret high above them, reflecting its buttery color into what little blue was left of the lake.

"Run!" Brittany said as Lee splashed furiously past her to get to the shore.

If the Headmaster had been looking out the window instead of into his cold teapot he would have seen seven figures kicking their way out of the lake and sprinting to a large van idling near the cafeteria. He might have seen how their chests expanded with laughter as they slapped each other on the back and screamed at their success. He might have seen, but he didn't.

It didn't matter that he hadn't seen it. The Headmaster did not need to consult his file of troubled students or conduct an investigation. Westbrook Preparatory had been his home for 43 years. He knew the land and the lake, the course schedules and the food in the cafeteria. He knew the people, and he knew the students. And so he knew that for something like this only one person could be responsible.

Mildred Dennall was a junior who was completely unexceptional in almost every way. She was of average height and body size. Her face was most commonly referred to as "good enough," and her body was set to stun not kill. Her grades were consistently lackluster C's, and her athletic ability was confined to short distance power walking. In short, she was the very definition of mediocrity.

But everything that happened of any interest at Westbrook was because of Mildred. Every classroom with rearranged furniture, every defaced painting and certainly every stray cat that wandered onto campus. The Headmaster was positive she was behind the day the homeless population of Virginia converged onto their campus thinking it was a soup kitchen. And though he had no proof, he also knew she was the one behind the underground spirit days, which were originally designed to celebrate Westbrook's history and now included activities that ranged from offensive to illegal. He knew this the same way he knew that God existed, not because he could prove it in any substantiated way, but because it was the only explanation that made sense. If Mildred Dennall didn't do it then it wouldn't happen.

* * *

The second day started with the lake glowing yellow and ended with the seven girls blindfolded in a circle. They had received their instructions through a far less exciting method this time, text messages from blocked numbers. The instructions had been to show up at the English building with a secret and a blindfold. When they arrived they had been escorted to the backs of cars and driven to an undisclosed location. Jennifer White was the only one who appeared relaxed.

"Share," Mildred said, and Shannon jumped because she had thought they were alone. "There are only two rules: it must be a secret you have never told anyone. The darkest, ugliest part of yourself. And once you share, no one can ask questions."

One by one they went, reaching their fingers out to scrape the frayed jeans of their neighbors and remind themselves that they were not alone.

"Rob and I had sex," Shannon began.

"Boring and not a secret," Mildred interrupted.

"In an airplane bathroom," Shannon finished in one dry exhale. Someone snickered, Other Jennifer shook her head, and Lee crossed herself.

"Thank you for sharing," Mildred said and squeezed the knee by her hand. "Next."

"I'm American."

"I sometimes wish I were a man."

"I cheated on my SAT and got away with it."

"I've never kissed anyone."

"My name isn't Jennifer."

"I knew about Hex before last night." The room remained obediently silent, but the slow raising of Mildred's eyebrow was something that could be felt with tangible intensity.

"I'll go next," Mildred finally said. "I'm afraid. I'm afraid of everything, all the time, always. Everything I do and have done, the pranks, the felonies, the initiations, have been because I am afraid."

"Thank you for sharing," Tara said.

"Thank you for listening," Mildred said. "Next."

Voices that the girls did not recognize began speaking from outside the circle. The unseen members spoke of childhood mistakes, high school embarrassments, and failures that seemed too large to navigate. When it was over they sat in the circle, hands loosely draped across the bodies of the girls on their sides, and even though the seven of them wore blindfolds and would soon be sitting in the back of a car with their heads down, even though one of them was there by accident and had to be gotten rid of, the only word they could use to describe the girls in that moment was sisters.

* * *

On the third day they got tattoos. If someone had been looking closely they would have seen the pale, white scarring scattered across their bodies in the shape of two interlocked triangles. The symbols lingered on the bottom of callused heels and behind over-pierced ears. Some lined the fragile skin of their hips and others the curve of a back.

Other Jennifer did not protest. She was the first one to go under the needle, her eyes fixed on the unforgiving fluorescent ceiling as a man whose hairy belly protruded from his shirt and rubbed her leg, marked her with permanent ink. She was the only one who did not whimper when they carved her skin.

Lee Sun refused to take off her headphones.

"I won't hear, I won't hear," she repeated until the man with the dough belly relented and let her keep them on. Tara took a shot of whiskey before stretching out in the chair. She handed the flask to Brittany who spit in it before giving it to Lauren.

"Are you crazy? Do you know what alcohol does to the body's defense mechanisms?" Lauren said and tossed the bottle to Shannon.

"No," Shannon said and took a long pull.

"You don't need defense mechanisms," Jennifer White said, slinging an arm around both of their shoulders. "You've got us."

* * *

The fourth day was not the scariest, but it was the most terrible. They were at Broan Lake again, blindfolded in a random formation with no concept of space or each other's proximity.

"Once a Hex, always a Hex, our bodies belong together." Anonymous voices from an outer circle chanted, their voices undulating and moving in a strange, spiritual dance. Brittany wondered if the other girls were even there. Shannon had talked about not coming back, but she was the kind of person who talked about a lot of things she would never do. She thought about Shannon and shin guards until she smelled Mildred's familiar toothpaste breath, followed by the sound of her deep, steady voice.

"Give me a piece of your body."

"What?"

"Give me a piece of you that I can keep. Something unnecessary."

Brittany looked through the slit of light at the bottom of her blindfold onto her flip-flopped feet and sighed in resignation. She kneeled down, peeled off a particularly long hangnail from her thickly calloused feet, and held it out in front of her.

"Not the most useful, but it will do."

The other contributions had been fairly standard: an eyelash or a thin strand of hair. Lee gave her headphones because she understood the meaning of sacrifice better than most. Tara dug a fingernail into a zit and let the pus ooze into the jar Mildred held out for her. Jennifer White was the snarkiest and pulled a gob of earwax from her ear and flicked it into Mildred's palm.

Brittany was proud of her contribution and stood in relaxed posture thinking the worst must have been over, which Lauren knew meant the worst was yet to come. When Mildred came back around with a spoon smelling of beach restrooms and used tampons, Brittany did not need to ask what to do. She took a sip and swallowed without gagging.

"Now you are a part of us," Mildred said. She lifted the blindfold, gave her a hug and smiled.

* * *

Compared to the others, the fifth day was rather simple. They were in the basement of a building without windows. They had to keep eating and not throw up. The foods weren't even gross, just juvenile. Buttered crackers, donuts, and rolls of cookie dough. After an hour Lauren's minuscule frame and bulimic tendencies got the better of her, and she puked all over the basement floor.

"Time," Mildred said. Shannon's body shook with sobs. She had not consumed this many carbs since meeting Rob.

"Years wasted," she choked out as she devoured another donut.

"You are one. When one throws up everyone throws up," Mildred said.

And so they did.

* * *

On the sixth day God created man, and the Hexes destroyed women.

"There are seven of you here," Mildred began. "There was never supposed to be seven. So get rid of one. Make sure she won't talk."

She left them in an abandoned warehouse with high ceilings and missing windows. The only light came from a bulb above their heads; it swung back and forth propelled by a gentle, moaning wind, sweeping them in and out of shadows. There were no blindfolds now, nothing to separate

137

them from the terrible truth of each other.

"Other Jennifer," Jennifer White said.

"No," Other Jennifer replied.

"Damn, I didn't think you'd put up a fight," Brittany said.

"You were never supposed to be here. You leaving makes sense," Jennifer White said.

"I have just as much right to be here as any of you." But her voice cracked in the middle.

"I'll go," Lee Sun said.

"No," six voices responded in unison. Lee Sun was one of them, there was no doubt.

"You could never keep me quiet. I'll tell everyone. I work for the school paper. How do you know I haven't been recording everything?" Other Jennifer said with remarkable calm.

"Because you're a coward," Shannon said from a pillar where she had been leaning quietly. "What? It's true."

"It is true," Brittany said. "But that doesn't mean she should go. I vote for Tara. She's so drunk she won't remember anything anyways."

"I remember," Tara's back rested against the cool concrete while her fingers flipped a lighter on and off. "I remember everything."

"Let's just vote and get it over with," Lauren said. She had been nervous after the vomit incident but was happy now to push attention away from herself.

"How many for Other Jennifer?" Jennifer White raised her hand and waited for them to follow.

"What about you, Jen? What about you? You're just another Jennifer," Shannon said. "I vote for Jennifer White."

"No," Jennifer said because she was still naive enough to think she had a say. "You can't take this from me. I won't let you."

"You're not going to let us do anything. We're just going to do it," Other Jennifer said.

And so they turned on her one by one, raising their fists without dropping their eyes.

"You can't keep me quiet. I'm no coward."

But it was six against one. It didn't take long for Lauren to brush the skin off Jennifer White's neck so Shannon could bring Tara's lighter to the sensitive skin behind her ear. They burned the small patch of skin behind her ear where her flesh was scarring so that the tattoo was indiscernible.

"You're not one of us," Brittany said.

"Never were," Tara said.

"And never will be," Lee finished.

"And if you ever talk about Hex," Other Jennifer (though she wasn't other anymore) knelt next to Jennifer White's quivering body and whispered.

"I don't understand," Jennifer White crouched with her hand over the twice-burnt skin behind her ear.

"This is how it works, Jennifer. This is how it has always been done."

* * *

On the seventh day they waited by the lake, skipping pebbles and rubbing the charred skin where the symbol for hex was scratched into their skin. They waited for a sign from the sisters they had fought so valiantly to join. But nothing happened on the seventh day.

Or the day after that.

Or the week after that.

Sometimes they met at Broan Lake and wondered. Sometimes they broke into Jennifer White's room to make sure she was still scared. They were well acquainted with the power fear had to bend a strong mind to its will.

It would have gone on like this forever if Lee Sun, in her shy, pocket sized glory had not heard the voice coming from a professor's office. She did not know Mildred's schedule or age or even her last name. But she knew the music of Mildred's voice with her eyes closed.

Once Lee shared Mildred's location, they decided to follow her home in Tara's mom's minivan, unafraid of the dark or of their questions. There were six of them, they were a part of each other and of Hex, and they would get what they wanted from her.

Mildred pulled into a damp alley behind an old restaurant and got out of her car.

"I figured something like this might happen," she said as the six of them approached.

"The game's up," Other Jennifer replied. "We found you, we did everything that you asked. We're Hex now."

"Oh, Jennifer." It was the first time Mildred had called her by her first name. "The game was that there was no game to begin with."

"It wasn't a game, it was our lives," Lauren said.

"I would have done it if I were in your place. I would have wanted to believe too," Mildred said, and Brittany thought how brave she was for looking them in the eyes the entire time.

"You would have done what, Mildred?" Shannon asked, but if she thought hard enough she could have guessed the answer.

"The only Hex played was on you, love," and then Mildred got into her car and left.

They stood in a circle similar to the one they had formed on the day they received their invitation, uneven and lumpy, but complete.

"This doesn't have to change anything," Tara said.

"There's nothing to change, Tara." Other Jennifer was swallowing tears, and her voice came out heavy and thick.

"We are part of each other," Lee said. Her headphones lay silent around her neck. "That will not change."

* * *

A year later there will be a similar occurrence. Haley Cruniksa might find a piece of paper in the pocket of a shirt she stole. Whitney Salen's will likely be rolled into a joint and cause her to choke. Courtney Rayne's will be written on the lucky $2 bill in her pocket and Rachel Mallack's calligraphied onto her favorite painting. Jamie Gade's will jangle from the hole in her guitar, and Sara Welsecky's will show up on her bank statement. The Other Sarah, Sarah Banrow, will find hers inside the pages of her locked diary.

There will be seven because that is tradition. They will drown in muck and dye a lake together. They will become irreparably connected, branded and bonded by the secrets they have shared. And on the sixth night they will cast out one girl and promise to burn her if she tries to talk.

They will do this because they must, because this is how it has always been done, because this is what it means to be hexed.

Winners of the Lamar University Literary Literary Press student writing contest for best short story:

First Place
"Dust" by Alaina Bray

Second Place
"Looking Inside Tulips" by Melissa Becker

Third Place
"The Guest" by Jaya Wagle